NOON CROUCHED IN THE CORNER, READY . . . WAITING . . .

"Now!" . . .

Three men leaped into the room; two through the windows, one through the door. That was their first mistake—winging from the bright sunlight into the dim room. All held guns, but only one got off a shot . . . and he fired as he fell, the gun blasting its bullet into the floor.

When the smoke cleared, Noon picked up the dead men's guns. He collected their horses and tied the gunslingers' corpses to them.

Before he sent them down the road, he pinned a tag on each. The tag read . . . "They tried to dry-gulch Ruble Noon!"

Bantam Books by Louis L'Amour

Ask your bookseller for the books you have missed

BORDEN CHANTRY
BRIONNE
THE BROKEN GUN
THE BURNING HILLS
THE CALIFORNIOS
CALLAGHEN
CATLOW
CHANCY
CONAGHER
DARK CANYON
DOWN THE LONG HILLS
THE EMPTY LAND
FALLON
THE FERGUSON RIFLE
THE FIRST FAST DRAW
FLINT
GUNS OF THE TIMBER-
  LANDS
HANGING WOMAN
  CREEK
THE HIGH GRADERS
HIGH LONESOME
HOW THE WEST WAS
  WON
THE IRON MARSHAL
THE KEY-LOCK MAN
KID RODELO
KILLOE
KILRONE
KIOWA TRAIL
THE MAN CALLED
  NOON
THE MAN FROM
  SKIBBEREEN
MATAGORDA
THE MOUNTAIN
  VALLEY WAR
NORTH TO THE RAILS
OVER ON THE DRY SIDE
THE PROVING TRAIL

THE QUICK AND THE
  DEAD
RADIGAN
REILLY'S LUCK
THE RIDER OF LOST
  CREEK
RIVERS WEST
SHALAKO
SITKA
TAGGART
TUCKER
UNDER THE SWEET-
  WATER RIM
WAR PARTY
WESTWARD THE TIDE
WHERE THE LONG
  GRASS BLOWS

Sackett Titles by
Louis L'Amour

---

1. SACKETT'S LAND
2. TO THE FAR BLUE
   MOUNTAINS
3. THE DAYBREAKERS
4. SACKETT
5. LANDO
6. MOJAVE CROSSING
7. THE SACKETT
   BRAND
8. THE LONELY MEN
9. TREASURE
   MOUNTAIN
10. MUSTANG MAN
11. GALLOWAY
12. THE SKY-LINERS
13. THE MAN FROM THE
    BROKEN HILLS
14. RIDE THE DARK
    TRAIL

THE MAN CALLED NOON

LOUIS L'AMOUR

BANTAM BOOKS · TORONTO · NEW YORK

THE MAN CALLED NOON

A Bantam Book | January 1970

2nd printing .... *February 1970*   3rd printing .... *June 1970*

New Bantam edition | May 1971

2nd printing .... *August 1971*	9th printing .... *July 1975*
3rd printing ...... *January 1972*	10th printing .... *May 1976*
4th printing .... *August 1972*	11th printing ..../.... *June 1977*
5th printing .... *March 1973*	12th printing .. *December 1977*
6th printing .. *September 1973*	13th printing ...... *March 1978*
7th printing .... *August 1974*	14th printing .... *July 1978*
8th printing .... *April 1975*	15th printing .... *June 1979*
	16th printing .... *April 1980*

ISBN 0–553–14203–8

Published simultaneously in the United States and Canada

Bantam Books are published by Bantam Books, Inc. Its trade-
mark, consisting of the words "Bantam Books" and the por-
trayal of a bantam, is Registered in U.S. Patent and Trademark
Office and in other countries. Marca Registrada. Bantam
Books, Inc., 666 Fifth Avenue, New York, New York 10019.

PRINTED IN THE UNITED STATES OF AMERICA

25 24 23 22 21 20 19 18 17 16

THE MAN CALLED
NOON

Chapter One

Somebody wanted to kill him.

The idea was in his mind when he opened his eyes to the darkness of a narrow space between two buildings. His eyes came to a focus on a rectangle of light on the wall of the building opposite, the light from a second-story window.

He had fallen from that window.

Lying perfectly still, he stared at the rectangle of light as if his life depended on it, yet an awareness was creeping into his consciousness that the window no longer mattered.

Only one thing mattered now—escape. He must get away, clear away, and as quickly as possible.

There was throbbing in his skull, the dull, heavy beat that was driving everything else from his brain. Impelled by what urge he could not guess, he lifted a hand toward his face. There was a twinge of pain from the arm, then he touched his face.

He did not know to whom the features belonged. Gingerly, he touched his skull . . . there was half-caked blood, and a deep wound in his scalp. His hand dropped to his shirt, which was stiffening with blood.

Somebody had tried to kill him, and he felt sure that they would try again, and would not cease trying until he was dead. Nothing else remained in his memory.

Stiffly, he turned his head, looking first one way and

then the other. In the one direction there was blackness, in the other was light . . . a street.

He was conscious of a faint stirring from the darkness behind the buildings. Something or someone was creeping along in the blackness, some enemy intent upon his destruction.

Heaving himself from the ground, he half fell against the building behind him. He remained there for a moment, struggling to gather himself for an effort. For he must escape. He had to get away.

A hand went to his hip. There was a holster there, but it was empty. Dropping to his knees, he felt quickly around him, but discovered nothing. His gun, then, must be up there, in that room. It had fallen or had been taken from him before he fell from the window.

He started blindly toward the street. He could hear music from the building beside him, a murmur of voices, then muffled laughter.

Staggering into the light, he paused and stared stupidly to left and right. The street was empty. Drunken with pain and shock, he started across the street and into the shadows of a space between the buildings diagonally across from the one he had left behind.

He had no idea where he was going, only that he must get away; he must be free of the town. Beyond the buildings between which he walked there were scattered outhouses and corrals, and a few lightless shacks, and then he was walking in grass, tall grass.

Pausing, he glanced back. There was no pursuit, so why was he so sure there would be pursuit?

He went on, his brain numb with the pounding ache, until he saw before him a single red eye. Staring at it, he went ahead toward the red light. Suddenly he was beside it and his toe stumbled against the end of a railroad tie.

To his left the rails glimmered away into a vast darkness, on the right they led to a small railroad station. He had taken a stumbling step toward it when he brought up short, realizing his enemies would surely look for him there.

He stopped, swaying on his feet, trying to order his thoughts.

He did not know who he was. Or what he was.

His fingers felt of his clothing. The coat was tight across the shoulders and the sleeves were a bit short, but it seemed to be of good material.

He glanced back at the town, but beyond the fact that it was a very small town it told him nothing. There had been hitching rails along the street, a few cow ponies standing there. Hence it was a western town.

He had heard the whistle a second time before it dawned upon him that a train was coming, and he would, if he remained where he was, be caught in the full glare of the headlight. He dropped into the grass not an instant too soon as the train came rushing out of the night.

A train offered escape, and escape would give him a chance to consider, to sort out what must have happened, to discover who he was and why he was pursued.

When the train had passed and drawn up at the station, he studied it with care. There were at least three empty boxcars, their doors invitingly open. Yet as he considered his chances of getting into the nearest one he heard a rush of horses' hoofs and twisted about from where he lay in the grass to see a party of horsemen dash up to the train and split into two groups to ride along both sides, checking every car, every rod and bumper.

He eased back further into the grass, but he could hear them talking as they drew near.

". . . a waste of time. He was in bad shape, with blood all over, and staggering. He could never have made it to the tracks, believe me. If he's not hid somewheres in town he's lyin' out yonder in the grass, bleedin' to death."

"He was a tough man for a tenderfoot."

"I ain't so sure he was—a tenderfoot, I mean. Ben Janish swore he'd got him, and did you ever know Ben to miss? That gent must have an iron skull!"

"Aw, he's dead, all right! Dead or dyin'."

They turned at the caboose and walked their horses back along the train. They were a dozen yards away when the whistle blew. Rising, he ran for the nearest empty car. A rider started to turn in his saddle, so he changed direction and leaped for the rear ladder and swung between the cars and out of sight.

He had a moment only until the cars would be moving, taking him right by the lights from the station, and he went up the ladder and lay down flat alongside the catwalk, throwing an arm across it to hang on.

The train bumped, started, bumped again, and gathered speed. Still he lay quiet, his heart pounding. Was somebody riding the caboose? Had he been seen from its windows?

The train whistled, the cars rattled over the rail ends and gathered speed. He pulled himself along, still lying flat, until he was right over the door of the empty car.

Did he dare try to hang over the edge, then swing into the door? If he fell he would fall free of the tracks, but could easily break a leg if not his neck. The train was now moving fast, the lights of the station had disappeared, and soon the brakeman would be coming along the catwalk, checking the train.

Easing along the roof of the car, he looked over. The door was there, open and inviting. He worked his body around, his fingers clinging to the cracks between the boards of the roof. He let one leg over, then the other, holding only by his fingertips. He lowered his body down, moved his hands one by one to a grip on the edge of the car roof, then swung his body in and let go.

He fell sprawling on the floor of the car, and for a moment he lay still, gasping for breath. After a long time he got up and staggered to the door. Leaning his shoulder against the car wall beside the door, he looked out into the night. There were stars, and the night was cool, the wind coming soft off the sagebrush.

He tried to think. Who was he? A fugitive from the law?

Or were those men who had tried to find him lawless men, wanting to kill him because of something he knew? Or because of something he possessed?

Sodden with weariness, he sat down and leaned against the wall, his body drained of strength, empty and sick. But he forced himself to think.

Ben Janish . . . he had one name, at least. Ben Janish had been sent to kill him, and Janish did not often miss. This implied that Janish was expert at the business, and might have killed before. They had spoken of him as a man with a reputation. Therefore it should not be too difficult to find Ben Janish, and find out who he himself was.

But if Ben Janish had been sent to kill him, he had been sent by whom?

They had said he was a tenderfoot, which implied he was new to the West. If this was the case, why had he come west? And where had he come from? Did he have a family? Was he married or single?

Well, he had the one clue. He must find out who Ben Janish was, and where he was.

He had no mirror, and therefore no knowledge of what he looked like. That he was tall was obvious, and by feeling his biceps he assured himself that he was an uncommonly strong man. Tenderfoot he might be, but he was no weakling.

He thrust his hands into his trousers pockets. One hand emerged with a small sack that proved to contain ten gold eagles and some odd coins. There was also a small but solid packet of greenbacks, but he did not take the time to count them.

The other pocket contained a strong clasp knife, a

white handkerchief, a waterproof matchbox, a tight ball of rawhide string, and three keys on a key chain.

The side pockets of the coat contained nothing at all, but the inside pocket paid off with some kind of legal document and two letters.

The letters were addressed to *Dean Cullane, El Paso, Texas*. Was that who he was?

He spoke the name aloud, but it evoked no response in his memory.

It was too dark to do more than make out the addresses on the letters, and he returned them to his pocket to wait for a better light.

"Well, Dean Cullane, if that is who you are, for a man with so much money you certainly have a lousy tailor."

El Paso ... he said the name but it meant nothing to him. However, it was his second lead. He would go to El Paso, go to the home of Dean Cullane and see if he was recognized there.

Yet ... did he dare?

Somewhere along the tortured line of his thinking, he dozed off, but was awakened when a rough hand grasped his shoulder.

"Mister"—the voice was low but anxious—"don't you swing on me. I'm a friend, and by the looks of that crowd waiting up the street, you need a friend."

He was on his feet, shocked into clear-headedness. The train was still moving, lights flashed past the doors, and they were entering a town. "What is it?" he asked. "What's happening?"

"There's a big crowd up the street, mister, and they've got a rope. They're fixing to hang you."

"Hang me? Why?"

"Don't stand there asking questions! When we pass that water tank, you jump and run." The man pointed toward a dark, looming building. "There's a gap between that building and the corral. You can take it running. At the end of the corral there's bushes, and right past the corner of the corral there's a path goes through into the wash.

"You take off up that wash for the hills, and if you can run, you'd better. Don't leave the wash until you see a big boulder, kind of greenish color, if it's light enough to see. When you get to that boulder you do a hard right and go up the bank. There's a path ... follow it."

The train was slowing now, and suddenly the man beside him dropped into the night, and was running. In an instant he had done the same. Even as he did so he wondered at the practiced ease with which he accomplished it. His memory might be gone, but the habit patterns in his muscles had not forgotten.

The water tank dripped into the dirt below, and there was a pleasant smell of dampness as he went past. He was aware briefly of the feel of cinders under his feet, the smell of coal smoke from the engine, and steam drifting back from the exhaust.

He saw the huge old barn, the corrals nearby, and he ran into the opening between, stretching his long legs and moving fast. The night was cool. He caught the fresh smell of hay and the smell of manure from the barns, and then he was past the corral.

Behind him men were shouting: "Search the train! Don't let him get away!"

He ducked into the black opening in the brush, was through it and into the sand of the wash. His running slowed because of the heavy going, but he plunged on until his heart was pounding so that it frightened him. He really slowed down then, walking and trotting. For a man who had been slugged on the head and who had been dead-tired a short time before, he seemed to have remarkable endurance.

He plodded on. The boulder loomed before him, and he turned and went up the bank. Almost at once he was on a path that ran parallel to the wash but a dozen feet above it, angling up the slope but under cover from the brush.

The trail dipped down to a small creek. He knelt and drank a little, and then as there seemed no other route he walked upstream in the water. He had gone no more than a quarter of a mile when a low call arrested him.

"Up here!"

He turned and went up into the rocks, where his unknown friend stood waiting.

Without a word the man turned and forced his way through a narrow crack in the rocks, followed a path for perhaps forty yards, and then ducked under some leaning boulders and into a small hollow among brush and huge rocks. He went through another crack and into a great cave formed by huge sandstone boulders that had fallen against each other.

A stack of firewood against one wall showed the place had been prepared, and there was a circle of stones and the blackened ashes and charcoal of old fires.

The stranger gathered sticks and commenced building a fire.

"Won't they smell the smoke?"

"Not much chance. Except the way we came, there's no way to get within half a mile of this place on horseback, and you know no cowhand is goin' to walk unless he's forced to. This hideout's been used forty years or more, and nobody the wiser."

From some unknown well of wisdom he said, "You just better hope no outlaw has turned lawman. It hapens."

The man had his fire going. He stood up, brushing his hands on his jeans. "Could happen," he agreed. He looked curiously at his companion. "My name is Rimes, J. B. Rimes," he said.

It was light enough to see him now. Rimes was thin, wiry, sandy-haired. His blue eyes were cool, shrewd eyes. Obviously he had expected his name to bring a response, but when it did not he threw the other an odd look, went back into a corner, and emerged with a coffeepot and cups. . . .

"You surely must be somebody, stirring them up like that," Rimes was saying. "I haven't seen so much action in that town since the last Injun raid . . . quite a few years back."

He said nothing because he had nothing to say. His head throbbed dully, and the reaction from his running had set in. He was dog-tired and bone-weary. But he was wary. He did not know this man who had befriended him, or why he had done so. He was grateful, but cynical. What did the man want? Who was J. B. Rimes?

"What do they want you for?" Rimes asked.

"It doesn't matter, really." How could he explain that he did not know why they wanted him? "I guess I was in the wrong place at the wrong time."

"It's your business. You got a name?"

"Call me Jonas. And thanks for helping."

"Forget it. Here, have some of this coffee while I have a look at that wound."

His fingers went to the cut on the head.

"I don't know what it was, either a bullet . . . or the fall I had."

"Bullet," Rimes said. "Somebody creased you."

He went to the corner from which he had taken the coffeepot and brought out a pan. Then he went to a corner in the rocks and filled the pan with water.

Suddenly the man who called himself Jonas was frightened. He thought he must have blacked out for a minute or two. Rimes must have gotten water and made the coffee . . . and then there was a blankness. He remembered his head aching, remembered Rimes getting the coffeepot. . . . He suddenly felt cold.

Had Rimes noticed? Would it happen again? Was it simply exhaustion, or was something wrong with his head?

"Odd wound," Rimes said; "looks like somebody was laying for you."

"Why do you say that?"

"He shot at you from above. Must have been in an upstairs window or on a balcony . . . maybe on a roof."

"Why not from some rocks?"

"You were shot in town."

Jonas was sharply aware of his empty holster. "Now how did you know that?"

Rimes glanced at him out of cool blue eyes that revealed nothing. "You came out of town, staggering and falling. I seen you a-comin'."

"You were at the station?"

Rimes chuckled. "That's not likely. No, I was sitting out in the tall grass, same as you, and just as anxious nobody would see me."

Rimes was bathing the wound with a damp cloth. "Cut right to the bone. Scraped it a mite, it seems like." He rinsed out the cloth. "Seems as if they've got you lined up, boy. When they hit you once, they hit you again."

"What makes you say that?"

"Old scar on your skull. Looks as if somebody had clobbered you before, sometime or other. This here bullet cut right across it just like somebody had aimed it."

An old scar? He might have many of them. He had no idea what he even looked like, let alone what scars might be on his body.

"Jonas . . . that's not a familiar name," Rimes commented.

"Maybe that's why I use it."

"Good a reason as any." Rimes squatted on his heels, stoking the fire. "Whoever shot at you didn't want to be seen. Figured you for a mighty dangerous man."

"I doubt it."

"It figures. There's a good many men running around who'd shoot you for fifty dollars, pick a fight and make it look all fair and honest where witnesses can swear it was a fair fight; so if they tried to ambush you they did it because they figured you'd shoot back, and fast."

He made no reply. The coffee tasted good, and when Rimes started frying bacon his stomach growled. He stirred uncomfortably.

"That empty holster worries me," Rimes said.

"I fell from a window, I think. I must have lost the gun when I fell, or a minute or so before."

"You don't remember?"

"No."

After a moment Rimes said, "I can let you have a gun. A man in your position had better go heeled."

Rimes went into the recess in the cave wall again and returned with a Colt and a box of shells. He tossed the gun to Jonas, who caught it deftly and spun the cylinder to check the loads, then holstered it.

"Well," Rimes said dryly, "you've used a gun before." He handed him the box of cartridges. "You may need these. I see you have some empty loops."

"Thanks."

The gun was new, a Frontier model, and the weight of it on his hip was comforting. "You trust me," Jonas commented.

Rimes's eyes wrinkled at the corners. "You need me," he said. "I don't need you."

"Yes?"

"Because, Mister Jonas whoever-you-are, you're playing it by ear. You don't know which way to turn. You don't know who your enemies are, or even if you have any friends, or where to find them if you do. You need me to bleed for information until you get yourself located.

"You're a lost man, Jonas. I've been watching and listening. I never knew a man so alert for every word

that might be a clue, or so jumpy at every sound.
Everything you say or do, you do as if you expected it
to blow up in your face."

"Supposing you are right? What then?"

Rimes shrugged. "I don't give a damn. I was just
commenting, and as far as you bleeding me for information, just go ahead, and bleed me. I'll help all I
can. After all, you'd help me."

"Would I?"

Rimes gave a faint smile. "Well, how should I know?
Maybe you wouldn't."

They ate the bacon from the frying pan, picking out
the strips with their fingers.

"What are you going to do?" Rimes asked. He was
interested, for this man had problems of a sort not
many would encounter, and as a man interested in
puzzles, he was curious as to what Jonas would do
now.

"Look for the pieces, and try to fit them together."

"Somebody wanted to kill you. They still want you
dead. Seems to me you're running a long chance, trying
to pick up those pieces. The first man you run into may
be one of those who are out to kill you."

"What about you?" Jonas asked.

"I sit tight. In a few minutes I am going to climb out
of there and set up a signal. The sun will catch that
signal and they'll read it off across the valley. Then
they'll come for me."

"And when we get where we're going?"

Rimes smiled thinly. "Why, there just might be
somebody there that knows you. It just might happen."
His smile widened. "That's why I gave you the gun."

Chapter Two

On the second morning he opened his eyes on a tiny band of sunlight that streamed through the smoke hole, which was itself a mere crack in the rock above the fire. He had worried about their smoke being seen until Rimes told him it was covered by brush and a cedar that leaned above it. The rising smoke thinned itself out and vanished in rising through the foliage.

Rimes was asleep.

For several minutes the man who called himself Jonas lay perfectly still, staring up at the ceiling of the cave. He felt restless and on edge. He was too close to his enemies, whoever they were.

The day of rest and thinking over his problem had brought him no nearer to a solution. He had no memory of his past. He had no knowledge of who he was, where he had come from, or what he was supposed to be doing there.

Well, the solution to that seemed simple enough. He must first of all discover his identity, and from that he would know all he needed to know. Or so he hoped.

Rimes had commented on it. "Bronc fighter I knew one time, he lit on his head and it was seven or eight months before he knew where he was, or who. But I've heard of others who came out of it very soon.

"And then there've been some," he had added slyly,

13

"who could remember but didn't want folks to realize it."

"That isn't true of me."

"You ought to tie in somewhere." Rimes was puzzled. "Of course, I've been out of touch, and I don't know of any outlaw outfit working this country except ours— and if there was a range war I think I'd have heard of it.

"You dress like a city man, but I've got a hunch you're not one. You might be a gambler who killed some citizen back yonder, but that wouldn't fit you being shot from ambush, if you were."

He had lighted his pipe with a stick from the fire. "What are you planning to do now?" he asked.

Jonas hesitated, wondering how much to tell; but this man had helped him, and seemed genuinely concerned.

"Did you ever hear of a man named Dean Cullane?" he asked.

Rimes's eyes were on his pipe bowl. When he looked up they were bland, too bland. "Can't say I have."

"Or Ben Janish?"

"Everybody knows Janish." Rimes drew on his pipe, then dropped the stick into the fire. "Seems to me you're remembering things."

"No, I heard them talking back there by the railroad. Probably there's no connection."

Now, lying upon his back in the cave, he considered the conversation. Had Rimes known Cullane's name? And if so, why had he concealed the fact?

The more Jonas considered his situation the more he wanted to be alone. He needed to get away to some quiet place, where he might recover some memories while not risking his neck by encountering unknown enemies.

He needed time to think, to plan, time to remember. Rimes had explained nothing. He had not told him where he was or where they were going; he had only implied that he might encounter an enemy there . . . or anywhere.

Was Rimes truly his friend? Or was he trying to learn something from him, some plan, some secret? How had Rimes happened there so opportunely? Of course, that could happen. Many men rode freight trains, and it was logical enough that they should help each other.

Rimes was no youngster. He was a man who had been through the mill. His advice to Jonas had been good. "Tell nobody anything. Say you had a run-in with the law, and let it go at that. Folks'll be almighty curious, being what they are, but if I were you I'd tell them nothing . . . nothing at all."

Rimes had taken him up the steep, winding stair, part natural, and part cut by hand, to where the signal mirrors were placed on the mountainside.

The valley below was relatively flat, semi-arid country, the hillsides dotted with cedar, the bottom largely sagebrush. Beyond lay a string of small mountains, actually low, rugged hills, broken by canyons and cliffs. "There's fifty trails going into those hills," Rimes commented, "and most of them just circle around, or go nowhere."

Jonas held up his hands and looked at them. What had they done? Why had men tried to kill him? Why, even now, did they search for him? Had these hands killed? Oh had they been used for some good purpose? Were they the hands of a doctor, a lawyer, a laborer, a cowhand? Had they swung a hammer or an axe? That they were strong hands was obvious.

He leaned back and closed his eyes. He might never discover his identity. He might be shot by the first person he saw; and if he was forced into a fight, what would he do? What manner of man was he?

The blow on his skull had wiped clean the slate of memory, so why not pull out now? Why not go far, far away and begin anew?

Yet how did he know that some memory, now in his subconscious, might draw him right back to the scene of his trouble? How could he go far away when he did not know in which direction to go? His enemies might be anywhere. What he had to do now was find out who and what he was.

He got up, tugged on his boots, and stamped his feet into them. He belted on his gun and reached for his hat.

"Well," Rimes said, "you're no cowhand. A cowhand always puts his hat on first."

Rimes threw off his blankets. "You go up on the lookout and see if you see anybody. I'll put some breakfast together."

It was bright and clear on the morning side of the mountain. He glanced across the valley, picked up a tiny cloud of dust, looked away and back again. It was still there, still coming.

Rimes came up to look. "It'll take them an hour to get here," he said, "the way they've got to come. Let's hang on the feed bag."

As they ate, Rimes explained. "Place we're heading for is a ranch. Owned by a girl whose pa just died a while back. Her name is Fan Davidge. Her foreman is Arch Billings. They are good folks."

"Running an outlaw hangout?"

"It's a long story. It's come to a place where they no longer can control it. Arch Billing is a fine man, but he's no gun-hand."

"Don't they have a crew?"

"Only man left is an oldster. The outlaws do the ranch work, and do it almighty well."

Together they gathered up, washed the frying pan and coffeepot, and stowed them away in the corner. By the time they reached the mountainside they could see a buckboard, only a mile or so off, and coming on now at a spanking trot.

There were at least two people in the buckboard. Rimes studied it through his field glasses. "Fan Davidge is aboard. Leave her alone."

"Is she somebody's woman?"

"No . . . but she's spoken for."

"By whom?"

They had started down the slope and they went six paces before Rimes replied, "Ben Janish."

"Is he the bull of the woods around here?"

"You bet your sweet life he is, and don't you be forgetting it, not for a moment. He won't be home right now, but Dave Cherry will be, and he's nearly as bad. You cross them and you won't last a minute."

The man who called himself Jonas considered that. "I am somehow not worried," he said after a moment. "I have searched myself and found no fear, but one thing I can tell you. I remember nothing, though, as I told you, I heard Ben Janish's name mentioned."

"So?"

"He was the man who shot me. He was hunting me."

Rimes stared at him. "You mean Ben Janish shot at you and *missed?*"

"He didn't miss. He just didn't hit me dead center. Rimes, you'd better leave me here. I don't know why Ben Janish wants me. I have no idea except that somebody must have paid him to kill me. Now I'd be a copper-riveted fool to ride right into his bailiwick, wouldn't I?"

The buckboard clattered up over the rock-strewn desert and came to a halt opposite them. The dust drifted back and started to settle, and J. B. Rimes walked down, greeting Arch Billing. Jonas was not looking at Arch, but past him, at Fan Davidge.

"There's little time," Billing said. "Mount up, boys."

"There'll be just one of us, I—" Rimes began.

"There will be two, Rimes. I am going along."

Rimes glanced at him, and then at Fan. "Your funeral," he said, and gestured toward the pile of blankets in the back of the buckboard. "Climb in, then. But you'd better be good with that gun."

The buckboard started off, and they went at a fast trot. Obviously Billing did not wish to linger in the area. Their presence in such a lonely place would be difficult to explain, as far off a reasonable trail as they were.

After a few minutes, Rimes asked, "Arch, is Ben in the valley?"

"No. He hasn't been around for a couple of weeks. El Paso, I reckon."

El Paso ... Dean Cullane's town.

The man who called himself Jonas, and who might be Dean Cullane, drew a blanket around his shoulders, for the wind was chill. He did not know who he was, nor where he was going, but now he knew why. He was going to the ranch because a girl lived there.

A girl named Fan ... who had merely glanced at him.

He was a fool.

Chapter Three

His hand touched his face. He was unshaved, of course, but there was a strong jaw, high cheekbones. There was quite a lot of money in his pockets, from what source he had no idea, and there were the letters and the legal document which he had not had the privacy to examine.

The buckboard had started off across the valley, but when it reached a sandy wash it descended into it, and turned at right angles. The going was slower in the wash, but Jonas thought they could not be seen because of the high banks.

There was no talking. Each of the occupants of the buckboard seemed busy with his or her own thoughts, and it provided time for Jonas to assay his position.

He knew he was a hunted man, hunted either by the law or by some individual with power. The fact that Ben Janish, whom he assumed to be an outlaw and a gunman, had been hired to kill him made it seem doubtful that it was the law that was seeking him. That such a man as Ben Janish seemed to be had been hired to do it made him assume that he was known as a dangerous man.

He now had three days' growth of beard on his face and letting it grow might be a good idea. It might help to conceal his features from people who knew him, at least until he knew them.

19

Several times they stopped to rest the horses, then went on. It was late afternoon when they drew up at a small seep and got down stiffly, stretching and brushing away some of the accumulated dust.

Arch Billing helped Fan Davidge down, and she went to a rock at the water's edge and dipped up water in a small tin cup and drank.

Rimes began putting together a small fire, and then, taking the gear from the buckboard, he made coffee.

Jonas sat on a rock apart from the others. The air was cool, and shadows began to gather in the hollows along the face of the hills. He heard a quail call ... a quail, or an Indian? There was no echo, no after-sound, and he knew it was no Indian.

How did he know that? Apparently it was only his name, his history, the actualities of his life that were missing. The habits, the instincts, the ingrained reactions remained with him.

Fan Davidge glanced at him, faintly curious. Men usually wanted to talk to her, but this one held himself aloof. He had a sort of innate dignity, and he did not seem like the others.

He was lean, but broad-shouldered, and altogether puzzling, resembling perhaps a scholar more than a western man; when he moved it was with the grace of a cat.

She watched J. B. Nobody knew more of what was going on than Rimes did. He had offered no explanation except to say the man's name was Jonas. Now he was crossing over to where Jonas was sitting.

Rimes spoke in a low tone, but the night was clear, and in the desert sound carries easily. She could just barely distinguish the words.

"If you want to light a shuck I can get you a horse."

"I'll come along."

"Look, if Janish is there—"

"Then I'll have some answers, won't I?"

"Mister, I don't know you, but I cotton to you. I don't like to see you get your tail in a crack."

There was no reply, and after a little while Rimes said, "Don't you think I don't know why you're taking this chance, but you'll waste your time."

"I had a feeling she was in trouble."

Rimes was silent for a moment. "Leave it lay. You'd just get yourself in a corner."

"I just got out of one."

"You're not out of it yet. Not by a long shot. If I only knew—"

"But you don't, and neither do I."

"Well," Rimes said after another pause, "there's two or three you'd better fight shy of. Dave Cherry . . . he's trouble. So's John Lang. And there will be others, so watch your step."

His head ached and he was tired, and he continued to hold himself aloof. He thought of the coming night, and was conscious of the faintest sounds, of the smells of coffee, of bacon frying, of burning cedar, and of sagebrush. He got up and walked off a few feet, feeling sick and empty, surrounded by unknown dangers.

A light step sounded behind him. It was Fan Davidge. "Please . . . you have been hurt," she said. "You had better drink this." She handed him a cup of coffee.

"Thank you." He looked straight into her eyes and liked what he saw there. He took the cup, and when she remained with him he said, "Don't let me keep you from your supper."

"You should eat, too."

But neither moved, and finally he said, "I like the twilight, but there is little of it in the desert."

"Who are you, Jonas? What are you?" she asked.

"I do not know." He looked at her over his cup. "I am afraid that what I am is not something to be proud of, but I do not know."

"What does that mean?"

He touched his wound. "That . . . since that I can

not remember. All I know is that somebody tried to kill me."

"You don't know who it was?"

"It was Ben Janish, but I don't know why?"

"*Ben Janish!* But then you mustn't come to the ranch! He might be there even now."

He shrugged. "A man will do what he must."

"But that's crazy! I mean . . ."

"There are two reasons, I guess. I had nowhere to go, and Rimes suggested the ranch. And then there was you."

"*Me?*"

"You looked to be in trouble."

She glanced at him. "You have troubles enough of your own."

Then she added, "I own the Rafter D."

Rafter D! Suddenly it was as if a shaft of light had stabbed into the darkness of his brain. He knew that brand . . . from where? How?

A thought formed in his consciousness. *Four to be killed . . . four men and a woman.*

Killed? By whom? And for what reason?

"You didn't know you were going to the Rafter D?" she asked.

"I didn't ask."

They walked back to the fire, and he refilled his cup and accepted a plate of food. The ache in his head had dulled, and the stiffness seemed to be leaving his muscles, but he still felt tired and on edge. The others sat about talking in a desultory fashion. They seemed to be waiting for somebody, or something.

He knew what was bothering him. He was afraid. Not of any man or men, but of discovering who and what he was. He would have liked just to walk off into the night and leave it all behind . . . all but Fan Davidge.

He did not want to leave her, and for that he felt that he was a fool, a double-dyed fool to be falling in love—if that was what it was—with a girl he scarcely knew and who was spoken for by the most dangerous man around. Why did that not worry him?

He went to the seep and rinsed his dishes, and replaced them in the buckboard. Arch Billing was standing near the horses, smoking his pipe. Rimes was dozing.

Jonas heard the faintest whisper of sound . . . listened . . . heard it again.

"Somebody is coming," he said.

Rimes opened his eyes, listened, then said, "I hear them."

There were two mounted men and they came up to the edge of the firelight. He could see little of their faces, but the firelight played on the horses' legs and shoulders, and he saw that one of the men wore Mexican spurs.

"Who's he?" the man asked, glancing at Jonas.

"On the dodge," Billing replied. "He came in with J. B."

Rimes stepped into the light. "Law was after him back yonder."

"I don't like it. I don't like him." The speaker was a big, rawboned man with a sandy walrus mustache.

"I don't give a damn what you like." The words came from Rimes. "I haven't asked you for anything, and there isn't anything you can give me."

The man on the horse seemed shocked, and his features stiffened. "The rest of you get into the buckboard and get started," he said. "We'll leave this gent right here."

"Now, see here, Lang," Rimes said. "I—"

"Thanks, J. B.," Jonas interrupted. He felt suddenly cold inside, and welling up within him was an ugly feeling. "Nobody needs to speak for me. If Lang wants to make an issue of it he can die here as easy as later."

John Lang was suddenly wary. For the first time he looked straight at the stranger. For a city dude, this one was pushing too hard. There had been rumors of hired killers being sent among the outlaws simply to kill.

"Nobody said anything about dying but you, mister," Lang said. "I just said we were going to leave you here. We don't know you."

"I don't know you, either, but I am willing to come along."

"Nevertheless, we leave you."

"No."

It was Fan who spoke, quietly but sternly. "This man has been injured. He needs rest and care. He is coming to the ranch with us."

Lang hesitated. He was a crafty man as well as a dangerous one, and he quickly saw this as an easy way out of a bad situation. After all, if need be they could always be rid of him.

"Certainly, ma'am. Whatever you say goes." He turned his horse and, followed by the other rider, disappeared into the darkness.

Fan started to get into the buckboard, and Jonas took her elbow, helping her in. She glanced at him, surprised, and said, "Thank you."

Billing took up the reins. Rimes tossed the last of their gear under the seat and got in. "You sure about this?" he asked.

The man who called himself Jonas shrugged. "I'm sure."

"You could have got yourself shot back there."

"I suppose."

"You sure don't seem worried."

"Why should I be? I'm wearing a gun, too."

Rimes had nothing more to say, and the buckboard was rolling, teetering over rocks, dipping down through a wash, emerging to wind a precarious way among gigantic boulders. The stars were out, the night was colder. Jonas hunched a blanket around his shoulders, eased his gun into a more favorable position, and dozed.

Twice they passed through small bunches of cattle. The only brand he glimpsed was a Rafter D. Once they went through a tiny stream, no more than a trickle of water.

Ahead of them, after they had traveled for some time, he heard John Lang call out: "It's all right, Charlie. It's the buckboard. We're bringin' in Rimes and a stranger. Says his name is Jonas."

"Just so's it ain't Jonah. But he better be advised. It's a whole lot easier to get in than to get out."

When Jonas helped Fan Davidge down she whispered to him, "Thank you . . . and be careful."

Rimes came up to him. "We'll go to the bunkhouse."

"Not yet," Jonas said.

Rimes paused, waiting for him to say more.

"What kind of place is this? Miss Davidge doesn't seem the kind who'd run an outlaw hangout."

"She doesn't run it. She just owns the ranch. Her pa built this ranch and turned it into a money-making outfit, but he was investing in other things, got rich, and went back east.

"He was an easterner, anyway, and he got to dealing with those railroaders and bankers back there. For a time he was a mighty well-off man, and used to come out every so often, then he came up short financially and died of a heart attack. Fan, she came back here to all that was left.

"Arch Billing ran the place for her pa when he was east, and Arch had rustler trouble. Friend of mine named Montana rode for him. Monty was a good hand, but not above holding up a stage or two if things looked right. He knew all the boys on the outlaw trail.

"Montana went to Arch and suggested he had some friends who could handle his rustler problem. Well, Arch knew they were outlaws, but they were also good cowhands when they wanted to work at it. They needed a place where they could lay low for a while, and Arch needed help with his rustler problem, so he took them on.

"Well," Rimes went on, "I was one of them. We just rode back to that rustler hide-out and laid down the law. We told them the Rafter D was friendly to us and we'd take it most unthoughtful if any more cattle showed up missing.

"Well, those rustlers were small potatoes, and they wanted no truck with the kind of shooting we would do, so they laid off. That day to this there's been no rustling of Rafter D stock.

"The thing was," he continued, "the first of us were mostly cowhands who'd got into trouble through brainless skyhootin' around. My first holdup was when I was seventeen—a bunch of us figured it would be smart to stop a train and pick up some drinking money.

"Well, we did it. We made the conductor give us twenty dollars and we were going to ride off and leave it at that. Then some wise jasper sticks his head out of a car and let go with a pistol. He hit Jim Slade, a friend of mine, gut-shot him. And I shot back, mad and not thinking, and I drilled that man through the skull.

"Nobody had figured on that. Nobody had thought it was anything but a lark; then all of a sudden it wasn't fun any more. Jim was dying, and that man I'd shot was a Wells Fargo agent. . . . I've been riding the outlaw trail ever since."

He lit his pipe. "The others were much the same sort, there at first, and we did far more punching of cows than riding the outlaw trail. This was home to us. No law came around, and we kept a good lookout. Arch knew what we were, but he ignored it, and then this other bunch came riding in."

"Ben Janish?"

"Him, Dave Cherry, John Lang, and some others. They'd held up a Denver & Rio Grande train and needed a hide-out. We didn't want their kind around, but we figured they'd pull out, and they did. Trouble was, they came back.

"Arch had this tough hand I was speaking about, the one we called Montana, and he braced Ben—told him they'd have to high-tail it out of there. Ben laughed at him, taunted him, and Monty went for his gun. Well, he never cleared leather before he had two holes right in the heart. Then Ben told us he figured to stay, and there wasn't a thing we could do about it.

"Fan's pa was alive then, and I know Arch wrote him about it, but Davidge died soon after, and that was an end to it."

"And then Miss Davidge came home?"

"That's right. Arch didn't like it, her being here with them, but there wasn't anything he could do about it. Whenever they ride off on a job they leave somebody here, and then Ben Janish let everybody know he figured to marry Fan so's he could tie up the ranch for good. And Ben let Fan know that if she tried to get away he'd kill Arch."

"Doesn't Fan Davidge have any family?"

"I've heard she has an uncle or a cousin, or maybe both. One of them lives down El Paso way, but they never cottoned to the old man, nor he to them, and they've never showed up. The uncle worked for Davidge in his office back east for a while, I hear. I wouldn't know anything about that."

Rimes seemed to have talked all he intended to, and he went with Jonas into the bunkhouse. There were bunks for at least twenty men, about seven of which seemed to be occupied. When Jonas followed Rimes into the room John Lang was standing before the fireplace, facing them.

There were two other men in the room with him, a sour-looking older man with thin white hair and olive skin. His eyes were black and shrewd. The other man, big, heavy-shouldered, and lantern-jawed, had a shock of blond hair.

It was this man who looked at Jonas. "I've seen you before," he said.

Jonas merely glanced at him, then picked up a worn magazine, and began to leaf through it.

"You!" The blond man pointed a stiff finger. "I'm talkin' to you."

Jonas looked up, let seconds go by while their eyes held, and then he said, "I heard you make some sort of a comment. I was not aware that it required an answer."

"I said I've seen you before."

Jonas knew trouble when he saw it coming, and he knew there were times when it was better to face it than avoid it.

"I don't recall seeing you, but I am sure that if I had I would remember the smell."

For an instant there was silence. Jonas had spoken so casually, in such an ordinary tone, that for a moment his words failed to register.

"*What* was that you said?"

"You seem to want trouble, so I decided to make it easy for you. I said you smelled—like a skunk."

Jonas was still half reclining on the bunk, and the blond man bent over, reaching for him. Jonas' left hand caught the sleeve on the reaching arm and jerked the man forward and off balance. The magazine, suddenly rolled tight, smashed upward, catching the attacker on the Adam's apple.

With a shove, Jonas threw the man off to the floor, where he rolled over, gasping and retching.

Jonas glanced at him, then opened the magazine, and began to read.

Chapter Four

The sour-faced old man, called Henneker, was forking hay into a manger when Jonas walked into the barn. He worked swiftly, silently, ignoring his approach. As Jonas turned to leave, the old man said, "He'll kill you. Kissling will kill you."

"Is that his name?"

"Yes. He's killed four men in gun battles. Maybe two, three others in holdups. You won't have a chance."

"Miss Davidge—does she like Ben Janish?"

"Her?" The old man straightened up angrily. "She wouldn't look at such as him. Only ever'body's afraid of him. Even Kissling an' Cherry."

"She's quite a woman."

"You bother around her an' I'll stab you with a hayfork. I'll come on you asleep. That's a fine girl."

"I believe you. She's the only reason I am here. When I saw her I had to come."

"She ain't for your kind."

"What kind am I?"

The old man strained up and looked at him with shrewd eyes. "Look, boy, I'm not as soft in the head as them in yonder. I know what you are, an' by comparison them inside ain't out of diapers yet. If I cared a plugged nickel for 'em I'd give warning, but they ought

29

to see they're nothing but a bunch of mangy coyotes with a lobo wolf among 'em."

The old man turned his back and started off, and the man who called himself Jonas stared after him.

Was the old man right? Was he worse than these men? Was he evil? If so, what was evil?

He shrugged and strolled to the corral to lean on the rail, watching the horses. They stirred warily, and his eyes were drawn to a line-back dun with black ears, black mane and tail.

The horse had stopped suddenly, ears pricked, and was looking at him. "Come here, boy," he said softly, and to his surprise, the dun came ... halted ... rolled his eyes, showing the whites, then sidled away. "It's all right, boy," he whispered, and held out his hand.

The dun's nose extended, sniffing the fingers.

"You have a way with horses, Mr. Jonas."

He turned to find Fan Davidge at his elbow. "That horse is an outlaw. Nobody has ever gotten so close to him before."

"He's your horse?"

"We brought him in with our stock off the winter range. He's a stray. I understand that's a Texas brand."

"Cherokee Nation," he said, and wondered how he knew.

She glanced at him curiously, but said only, "Ride him if you like ... if you can."

"Is he in anybody's string?"

"No."

He turned to look at her. "You are a very beautiful girl, Miss Davidge."

She flushed slightly. "Thank you."

Abruptly she turned and went back to the house. Whatever she had come to say, she had changed her mind. He watched her go, admiring her easy walk and the swirl of her riding skirt.

He had no right to think of this girl. He would be

inviting trouble he could not afford. And he had no idea who he was or what he had been.

Rimes came out of the bunkhouse. "Did you eat yet?"

"No."

"Come on."

Together they walked to the ranch house. The long room where the table stood opened off the kitchen. There were flowered curtains at the windows, and plants arranged in clay pots. Everything was bright, clean, attractive.

The cook, who was Chinese, brought dishes to the table, then returned to the kitchen. There was no sign of Kissling. Glancing to his left, Jonas saw a door opening to a room with shelves of books.

"Don't worry about Kissling here," Rimes said, speaking softly. "There'll be no shooting on the ranch. Her orders, and his—Ben Janish, I mean."

Presently Jonas said, "I think I will take a ride after I eat."

"Then go toward the mountains," Rimes said. "If you know anything about punching cows, ask Henneker what to do. Arch rode out this morning. We all help with the ranch work," he added.

"Suppose I just kept on riding?"

"You'd get nowhere. That's a wall of mountains yonder. There's fifty box canyons, all of them dead ends. You could climb out afoot, but there's nowhere to go. There'd be fifty or more miles of the roughest country in the world ahead of you . . . and no grub."

"I've got to find out who I am."

Rimes was silent a moment. "Leave it lay. Why don't you just start off as if you'd just been born? 'Let the dead past bury its dead,' as somebody said one time."

"The dead might not want to be buried, nor the past want to have them buried. I have an uneasy feeling about that."

Rimes talked of the ranch, the cattle. There had been no beef shipped from here since Davidge died, but the range was good. The mountains and the ridges formed almost natural corrals, and the outlaw hands had kept others away. There were thousands of acres between the ranch and the mountains, a restricted range, well-watered and in some cases sub-irrigated by the flow off the mountains.

Rimes left, and Jonas lingered over his coffee, worrying about his problem. Did Henneker know anything? Or was the old man just guessing?

There were clues . . . one was the recognition of the dun's brand as from the Cherokee Nation, which was an outlaws' hangout. The one thing he was sure of was that Ben Janish must know who he was and why he was to be killed.

And there were the letters and the legal document in his pocket, which so far he had not had a chance to examine.

Was he Dean Cullane? The letters he had found in his pocket, addressed to that name, would make it seem so, but somehow he was uneasy over the name. Might he have stolen them? Or offered to carry them for Cullane? None of the reasons he could think of made much sense.

He was feeling restless. His headache had dulled to a persistent throb that kept him on edge, and he was in no mood to be with people. He needed to get off by himself, to think, to plan, to try to find a way out.

Ben Janish would soon be coming to the ranch, and Ben would no doubt try to finish what he had begun. But what would be his reaction when he found the man he had tried to kill waiting for him?

Fan came into the room. "If you want to ride and you think you can handle that dun, you might check out my beef for me. I'd like to get an idea what there is that's ready to ship."

"I don't know," he said, rising. "I don't know what I know about cattle. Or even if I can ride."

"If you can ride that dun you're a better man than Kissling or Cherry. He threw both of them."

Several spare ropes hung in the blacksmith shop which occupied a corner of the barn. He chose one and went to the corral. Could he use a rope? It felt natural in his hands, and he supposed he could.

Rimes was close by when he let himself into the corral and faced the horses. They circled warily, keeping away from him.

He looked at the dun and held out his hand. "Come here, boy," he said, and the dun came.

"Well, I'll be damned!" Rimes muttered. "I never saw the like."

Kissling had come out of the bunkhouse, and he stood watching. Henneker, who had come riding up on a sorrel pony, stopped near Fan. "Now there's a funny thing," he said to her. "That horse knows him."

"But how could it? He just got here, and that horse was a stray we picked up on the winter range."

"Sure, I brought him in," Henneker said dryly, "but I still say that horse knows him. Ma'am, something's wrong here, almighty wrong."

The old man looked down at her suddenly. "Don't you go gettin' any case on that man, ma'am. He's a bad one."

"The dun doesn't think so," she replied.

Henneker snorted, and rode toward the corral.

The man who called himself Jonas walked the horse out of the corral holding its mane, then saddled up. As he moved he tried just to be guided by those automatic movements that seemed not to have been affected by his accident.

When he had finished saddling the horse Fan Davidge had come up close behind him. "Jonas, who are you? Why are you here?" she asked.

She had spoken in a low tone, and he responded in

the same way. "You know as much as I do. As far as I know, my life began half an hour or so before I got on the train where Rimes found me. That's all I know."

When he had mounted the horse he rode off without the dun so much as humping its back. She watched him go, sitting erect in the saddle, a handsome figure of a man. Then she walked back to the house, where Arch Billing was waiting.

"Arch, you don't suppose he's a government man?"

"How could that be?"

"Wells Fargo might have trailed some of them. He might be a United States marshal. He told me the dun's brand was from the Cherokee Nation."

"You mean you think he's one of those Judge Parker gunslingin' marshals workin' out of Fort Smith? That's a long way off."

"He could be from Denver or El Paso."

"Don't you believe it. Ma'am, he's a bad one, and I'd stake my life on it. Did Hen tell you what he did to Kissling?"

"Kissling had it coming."

"It was the way he did it. Like a man slapping a boy around. Kissling didn't worry him, not for one minute. He never even got to his feet, and he nearly killed the man. And you know something else? He didn't care. He just didn't care one way or t'other."

For several minutes neither spoke, and then it was Arch who said, "We've been used by Ben Janish and his outlaws, so maybe we can use this stranger. Maybe this man is the one to rid us of Janish."

"How?"

"He's a loner. You can see that. He came out here for something, we don't know what, but he don't care whether school keeps or not. The way he sizes up to me, he's the kind would charge hell with a bucket of water."

"Ben Janish would kill him."

"And he might kill Janish. They might even kill each other."

"Is that what you're hoping?"

"Ma'am, I never had no family. None but you and your pa. All I want is to see you with this here ranch and free of them. I'd like to see you with a man ... the right kind of man."

"Thanks, Arch." After a pause she said, "I don't want him killed."

He looked at her. "Ma'am ... don't. He's a bad one. I can tell."

"Just the same, I don't want him killed."

The man who called himself Jonas rode toward the mountains. He reached for the gun in its holster and it slid easily into his hand ... too easily.

He reholstered the gun and thought about his problem. There had to be a record. When a man turned up missing inquiries were made—unless he was one of those footloose ones with nobody to care. But somebody, somewhere, would know.

He was feeling better. To wait here for Ben Janish was foolish. What he must do now was to get away, to find out something about himself, to discover who he was and why he had been where he was, and why Ben Janish had tried to kill him.

He rode across the flat valley floor, where the pasture was good. The stock he saw was in good shape, much of it ready for shipping, but it was high time some of the older stuff was moved out.

There was plenty of water in the several streams running down from the mountains, and he could foresee only two problems for the ranch. The first was the necessity for shipping. Unless the older steers were moved out and sold soon, the range would be overstocked and soon overgrazed. The second problem was the question of winter feed. Unless a lot of hay was cut they were going to have a time getting through the winter.

On thin snow most of the stock would do all right. They would be able to get at the grass for limited grazing, but if there was any kind of a fall of snow the canyons would be snowed in and much of the range would be covered too deep. The outlaws were good hands up to a point, but they had no interest in the cattle, and they did not relish the idea of cutting and stacking hay—hard work at best.

Nevertheless, with a few hands and some supervision the ranch would be a good operation. Because of the natural fencing offered by the mountains the stock could be controlled with no difficulty. Only at roundup time would they need outside help.

The dun was a fast walker, and they were making good time. Looking ahead he could see no way out for a man on horseback, and only a possibility for a man afoot. The mountain before him rose in a rugged, tree- and brush-clad slope so steep a man would have to cling to the brush to climb up its side.

When he came close to the mountain he turned the dun and rode along its base, studying the ground. If there was a way out, some of the stock would have found it, or at least wild animals would have done so. He had seen a few deer tracks ... where had they come from?

Deer, unless driven by fire or by drought, will rarely get more than a mile or two from the area where they are born. Usually they sleep in an open place somewhere up on a slope, and shortly before daybreak they feed down toward water, drink, idle about a bit, and gradually feed back up the slope. This valley might be home to them, but they might have found a trail to somewhere high up on the mountain.

Riding a horse alone, as Jonas was doing now, was a time for thinking, and again his thoughts returned to his problem. The questions remained. Who was he? What was he? Where was he from?

Although he had no memory, he realized that he did

have his habit responses, and this could offer a clue. Suppose he began to test himself little by little, trying different things to find out the range of his skills?

He had already discovered that if he let himself go without trying to direct his actions he functioned fairly well. When he had saddled the dun he deliberately allowed his muscles free rein and he had worked with practiced ease. And now he thought about the dun.

Why had the horse come to him so easily? Had he known the horse before? Had it, perhaps, belonged to him at some time? He remembered that the old man, Henneker, had said he was a bad one. Was he? Searching himself, he could find no such motivations. He felt no animosity toward anyone, nor any desire to do evil.

Yet, did evil men ever think of themselves as evil? Did they not find excuses for the wrong they did?

He noticed the deer tracks without paying much attention, his thoughts busy elsewhere. Only when a second set of tracks joined the first did his mind really focus on the matter. Deer were creatures of habit, he knew, more so than men. The tracks of the first deer were several days old; the tracks of the second had been made that morning.

They disappeared suddenly, near the mouth of a canyon, but search as he might he could not find them entering the canyon. Knowing, from some bygone store of knowledge, that quite often a human or game trail will skirt the edge of a canyon, he rode back and studied the approaches to the canyon.

At first he found nothing, but he persisted, and after nearly an hour of searching he found where a vague trail went between two close-set clumps of cedar, rounded a boulder that appeared to block any progress in that direction, and went upward under the pines.

It was at that moment he thought of the letters.

Chapter Five

He drew up in the shade of some pines near the trail and took the letters from his pocket. Both were addressed to *Dean Cullane, El Paso, Texas*. The first was short and to the point.

> The man I am sending is the best. He knows what to do and how to do it. Do not interfere or try to communicate with him.
>
> Matherbee

The second letter, posted a few weeks later, was from the Pinkerton Detective Agency.

> Our investigation has, I regret to say, been inconclusive. The man of whom you require information first appeared in Missouri, where he was reported to have arrived on a freight train. He worked there for a tie-cutting camp, where he became involved in a brawl with two men, who were beaten severely. The first shooting of which we have record took place a few weeks later in a saloon when a trouble-hunting outlaw from down in the Nation started a fight.
>
> Both men went for their guns, and the outlaw, who had quite a reputation, came out a poor second. It is reported that a cattleman was in

the saloon, saw the action, and later had a talk with the man you are interested in, whose name is reported to be Ruble Noon.

The next day Noon bought a complete outfit, including a horse and several hundred rounds of ammunition, and then he drifted.

Stories get around. The report is that this cattleman had been having rustler trouble, he had lost stock, and one of his hands had been murdered after apparently coming upon some brand blotters. That was in western Nebraska.

Ruble Noon was not seen around, but a few days later one of the rustlers was found dead in his cabin, a gun in his hand that had been fired once.

A few days later two of the others were found dead on the plains covered by the hide of a steer with a brand half blotted. Both men were shot from in front, both were armed.

A few days later the last of the rustlers, three in number, were seated at their fire. They were in possession of thirty head of stolen cattle.

A man stepped from the trees about sixty feet away. He said, "I am Ruble Noon, and I killed Maxwell."

They'd been saying what they would do if they caught him, and he had come to them. They went for their guns. Two died before they could get off a shot, but the third, one Mitt Ford, got into the brush, tried a shot from there. The answering shots burned his shoulder and wounded him in the side, and he got away, fast.

Mitt Ford told the story. He had not got a good look at Noon, for he was standing against a wall of tall trees, his hat pulled low. All Mitt could say was that he was tall, slim, and hell on wheels with a gun.

There was an express company up Montana way. Too many holdups. They hired Noon. When the next holdup took place somebody shot from the brush and there were three dead outlaws. No more holdups on that line.

There was more. He scanned the report with care. Ruble Noon had apparently only one contact, the cattleman who first hired him. This man acted as go-between in every case, and there had been a dozen more cases, from Canada to Mexico. There was no description beyond that given by Mitt Ford, and the tie-cutting outfit had scattered. The cattleman claimed to know nothing about him.

There was one final note. The cattleman in question had at one time made a cattle drive with Tom Davidge. They had been friends.

Ruble Noon folded the letters and returned them to his inside pocket. The legal document was a deed to three hundred and twenty acres of land and a cabin; it was made out to Ruble Noon and signed by Tom Davidge. Appended to the document was a small hand-drawn map showing how to get to the property.

The dun was growing restive, and he started on, knowing no more about himself than before.

The letters and the document had been in the possession of one Dean Cullane, of El Paso, whoever he was. Why did Cullane have a deed destined for Ruble Noon? Were Cullane and Noon the same man? It seemed doubtful.

Was he Cullane? Or was he Noon? Or was he neither one?

Slipping off the coat he was wearing, he checked it with care. The sleeves were too short, and the shoulders too narrow, though not by much. The coat was tailored, not a ready-made.

"Tailored," he said aloud, "but not for me." He knew he would never have accepted a coat that fitted so badly. If the coat was not his, it must be Dean Cullane's, for the letters were addressed to him. . . . Or could the coat belong to Ruble Noon? For the deed had been there, too.

Was there any way in which he could discover who Ruble Noon was? Or Dean Cullane? Or Matherbee?

He looked again at the map. Only a few lines on a bit of paper, but that X might be this very ranch, and the dotted line could be that faint trail he had discovered.

Why had Ruble Noon a ranch in the area? What was his connection with Tom Davidge? He had no answers —nothing but questions.

He was hungry, and he had not thought to bring food with him. But he did not want to go back now. There was too much to think about, too much to decide. And he did not know what awaited him back at the ranch . . . Ben Janish might have returned, and it was Ben Janish who had tried to kill him.

He swung his horse around, returned to the trail, and turned the dun up the mountain. After a dozen quick, tight turns they began to wind through the forest, climbing steadily. The mountain was steep, but the deer had found a way to the meadows below. There were no horse tracks on the trail, only those of deer.

He kept on, studying the country as he rode. The growth was so thick that only occasionally could he see the ranch or the valley below him. He followed the dim, narrow trail back and forth up the steep scarp until suddenly a notch in the mountain, invisible from below, opened before him.

The dun went forward slowly, ears pricked with curiosity. The notch opened after some hundred yards into a long trough down which a stream ran. It was high grassland, the slopes covered with pines, and about a quarter of a mile away he could see a small cabin, perched on a shelf among the trees.

There was no sound, nor any sign of life there.

Above on the mountain a rock cropped out, bare and cold against the sky; below it only a few straggling pines, wind-torn and twisted, stretched black, thin arms against the sky.

It was a lonely place where the shadows came early and where cold winds blew off the ridges. Who had found this spot? Above all, who had thought to build here, under the bleak sky? On any cloudy day the place must be filled with damp, clinging gray clouds, and thunder must roll down this narrow valley, leaving the air charged and smelling of brimstone. It was a place of bitter solitude ... yet somehow it appealed to him, somehow he knew this was his place, where he belonged.

The only sound was that of the dun's hoofs in the tall grass, and occasionally the click of a hoof against stone.

He went up the trail to the shelf and stopped before the cabin.

It was built against a wall of rock, sheltered half beneath the overhang, and was of native stone, the cold gray rocks gathered from the foot of the cliff. It had been built a long time ago.

No mortar had been used, only stone wedded to stone, but cunningly, skillfully done by the hands of a master. The stones had taken on the patina of years, and the heavy wooden bench made of a split log was polished as if from much use. A stable backed against the wall where the fireplace stood so heat from the fire would help to warm the stable. A passage led from the house into the stable, and a stack of wood stood high against the stable walls.

Dismounting, he tied the dun to a post and went up to the door. It opened under his hand, and he stepped in.

He had expected nothing like this. The floor was carpeted with skins, the skins of bear and mountain lion. There was a wall of books, a writing table, and a gunrack holding a dozen rifles and shotguns.

In another smaller room there was a store of canned goods and other supplies. These things had never arrived over the trail by which he had come; therefore there must be another and better route.

Somebody had lived here, perhaps lived here still, and that somebody was probably Ruble Noon, for this must be the cabin deeded to Noon by the document he carried.

He walked to the windows. The view from them covered all the valley below. The only blind spot lay on the steep mountainside above the cabin, a place from which one might come to the cabin unseen. Otherwise the only access to it was by coming up from the front.

After studying the view he sat down in the chair at the desk. It was a comfortable chair and felt right to him, and the cabin felt right, too. In the winter this valley would be snowed in, closed off to the world, but in the summer it was a haven, a secure place.

He got up suddenly. He must be getting back. In actual distance he was not far from the Rafter D, but at the pace he would have to travel it would probably take almost two hours to return.

But first he must discover the other way into the high valley. A careful search proved only one thing: there was no easy way out of the valley, and in fact no way at all that he could find. Yet there had to be such a route. Nothing that was in the cabin could have been brought up the way he had come.

For the first time he stood back and studied the rock-built cabin itself. Immediately he was aware that a part of it was much older than the rest. The stable and part of the cabin had been added at a later date, but that part of the stable that adjoined the house was older.

But he realized that he could spend no more time here at present. Mounting his horse, he went back the way he had come, pondering the problem of the access route. When he had once more come to the bottom of the steep mountainside he remained under cover for some time, studying the surrounding area to be sure that nobody saw him emerge from the trees. Then he swung down and carefully removed as many traces of his passage as possible.

The moon was up and supper was long past when he rode into the ranch yard. As he dismounted he saw a man stand up and go into the bunkhouse. Was it Kissling, watching for him?

He stripped the gear from his horse and turned the dun into the corral, then went up to the ranch house. The Chinese cook had finished washing up and showed no pleasure at seeing him.

"Supper all finish," the cook said. "What you want?"

"Coffee will do—just coffee."

Fan appeared in the door from the study. "You go ahead, Wing. I'll find something for him."

Grumbling, Wing went off to his quarters, and Fan brought some bread, cold beef, and cheese from the cupboard. "There's some frijoles, too," she said. "Do you want them?"

"Please."

"Have a nice ride?"

His way of answering was to say, "You've got some cattle that must be shipped. I'd say four or five hundred head, but there might be twice that many."

"We haven't shipped any cattle since pa died. Even since before he died."

"You're overstocked. The range is in good shape because you had plenty of rain and snow. But it won't be good next year until you get rid of some older stock."

"I don't know whether Ben Janish will let us."

He glanced at her. "The hell with him."

"That is easy to say. We would have to have extra hands . . . most of these boys don't dare appear where the law can see them. Word would get out, and this place would be ruined for them."

"Did you ever hear of a man named Matherbee?" he asked.

"No."

"How about Ruble Noon?"

"Everybody knows about him."

For a few moments then they sat in silence while he ate. She refilled his cup.

"Apparently I have forgotten much," he said. "Or perhaps there was much I never knew. Put yourself in my place. I do not know what kind of man I have been, nor how I should react. I know that men were wanting to kill me, but I do not know if they were a mob or the law. I sometimes think that I should go away from here, lose myself in the mountains, and stay there until my memory comes back and I know who and what I am."

"I would miss you," she said suddenly, without thinking.

"Those are the first kind words anyone has said to me, but don't think them. Neither of us knows what I was, nor what I will be if my memory returns. I am a haunted man—haunted by the ghosts of what I may have been."

"Then make a decision to start over," she said. "No matter what you have been, you can always become something else."

"Is it that simple? Is a man ruled by his own free will, or is he a composite of all his experiences, his education and heredity? I may not know what I am, but my flesh and blood do know, and they react the way they have been conditioned to react. My conscious mind was born only a few days ago, but the habit patterns built into my muscles have forgotten nothing."

"I cannot believe you were bad."

"Don't gamble it. When Kissling attacked me I did not think. Whatever I did, it was in me to do."

"What will you do now?"

He shrugged, and finished his coffee. "Ben Janish will be coming back, and if he is gunning for me I must kill him or be killed. They say he is an expert, and I do not know whether I can even shoot straight."

He got up. "I think I will go away for a while. I will try to find out something about myself—who and what I am. If it is something worthwhile, I will come back."

"I would like that."

For a few minutes they talked quietly, and then he excused himself and went outside. The night was cool and quiet, and he stood very still, listening to the night sounds and breathing deep of the fresh air. But there was no quiet in him, there was only torment. Still the same questions: Who was he? What was he?

There was something within him that responded easily and naturally to Fan Davidge. He was at ease with her, he felt right with her; but at any moment his whole life could blow up in his face.

What if he was an escaped criminal? What if he was wanted by the police for some crime?

And who was Matherbee? Who was "the man who was best for the job"? Who was Ruble Noon? Or Dean Cullane?

He knew he must go to El Paso. But first he must return to the cabin in the mountains, search it for some clue to Ruble Noon, and then find the other way out. Then it would be time to go to El Paso.

If he lived that long . . .

Chapter Six

The last stars of night clung to the sky, and there was a growing light in the east when he rolled silently from his bunk and dressed. He was outside when he heard a faint step. It was Henneker.

The old man stared at him sourly. "Pullin' your freight?"

"Yes."

"What about her?"

"You told me she wasn't for my kind. Maybe you're right."

"I don't mean that. I mean Ben Janish. He was your job, wasn't he?"

The man who called himself Jonas tightened a strap. There was something here he did not understand.

Henneker spoke impatiently, keeping his voice low. "Arch doesn't know a thing, but the old man talked to me. I told him you were the only man for the job. He already knew of you, though, and I think he'd been studying on it. I think he knew when he left that he'd never come back, so he had to decide."

"I don't know what you're talking about." The morning was cold, and he wanted to be away before any of the others were around.

"All right," the old man said testily, "you don't know anything, and if anybody asks me, neither do I, but if that girl's to have any decent kind of life you'll have to do what you was paid for."

"And what was I paid for?"

Henneker snorted. "I told you Davidge talked to me. Four men—that's what you was paid for, four men who needed their hair lifted. You was paid for Dave Cherry, John Lang, Cristobal, and Ben Janish."

"Why didn't he include Kissling?"

"He wasn't here at the time. Anyway, he's small stuff. I could handle him myself."

"You?"

Henneker stared at him. "I never taken up your kind of work as a business," he said. "I done it for a hobby. Although," he added, "I don't figure I was up to Ben Janish even when I was a kid. Maybe Wes Hardin could do it."

"You think I can?"

Henneker shrugged. "You taken the money. You got the job. You do it in your own way an' your own time . . . only time is runnin' out."

Jonas swung into the saddle and reined the dun around. "I'll be back," he said, and walked his horse away into the night.

Behind him he heard a door close and John Lang's hard voice. "Who was that?"

"The stranger," Henneker answered. "He's goin' out to tally cattle."

Jonas drew rein, listening. After a moment Lang said, "Well, he won't do no harm. He can't get past Kissling, anyway. He's at the gate."

Once away from the ranch, he put the dun into a gallop. This time the trip to the cabin took less time, even with the extra precautions he took. At the cabin he stabled the dun, and taking a scythe from the wall, cut enough grass for the horse to keep busy.

The builders of this cabin seemingly had prepared for anything, and he felt sure they had planned a way out of this high valley as well. The larger part of the structure was old, and it was that part built under the overhang that was oldest. He wanted to find what lay behind the cabin, beyond the rock knoll against which it was built.

He scrambled to the top of the rock, and walked over it toward the far side. He stopped so suddenly that he almost fell. Before him the rock dropped sheer away for several hundred feet. Far below him he glimpsed a dim trail that seemed to point toward the rock on which he stood.

Suppose that trail dead-ended against the cliff? Suppose there was some way up from within the rock? The rock dropped so steeply that to go further was to risk a fall, although a man in his socks might work his way down to the lip of the overhang, the chance was too great.

He went back down to the cabin, keeping the distances in mind. Obviously, the back of the house must be within a few feet of the face of the cliff. Had there been a wind-hollowed opening there before the cabin was built? There were many such "windows," as they were called in this country, in Utah, New Mexico, and Arizona, as well as in Colorado.

Inside the cabin he looked around slowly and carefully. In his earlier examination of the place he had given only a few glances around. He had sat in the chair, but he had not taken time to look at the books or to examine the guns—to open the door of the closet . . . doors, he should say.

He opened them, and there, in neat rows, hung half a dozen suits, several pairs of jeans, several kinds of boots, and half a dozen hats of different styles. Whoever had used this place had evidently wanted to alter his appearance from time to time. Suddenly his eye was drawn to something on the floor of the closet . . . sand.

From the boots?

Shoving the clothing aside, he saw there a small

door, which was not over five feet high and four feet wide.

His hand felt for the almost concealed latch and swung the door outward. A cool breath of air fanned his cheeks. He peered through into a cavern and saw, some thirty feet away, an oval of blue sky.

He stepped through the opening, and saw at one side of the cave a winch and ropes that hung into a hole. He bent over and looked down.

It was a chimney in the rock face, varying from about four feet wide at the top to ten at the bottom. Suspended in it was a crude platform about three feet square that could be raised and lowered by the windlass.

This, then, was the way in which supplies were brought to this place and the way in which access could be gained from the outside. Once up here, and the platform pulled up, there would be no way to reach the cabin, even if anyone knew it was there. No more perfect hideaway could be found anywhere.

What about a horse?

It was likely that the man who used this hideaway kept horses at both places, in the valley below and up here. Yet there was no evidence that whoever had stayed here had ever used the trail to the Rafter D, and it was sheer chance that he himself had found it.

Once more he sat down to think things over. Slowly his mind went back over his conversation with Henneker.

The old man had obviously mistaken him for somebody else . . . or had he? Suppose he was a hired killer, hired by Tom Davidge to rid himself and his daughter of the men who had moved in without invitation, and had remained?

Suppose . . . just suppose that he himself was Ruble Noon? Suppose his finding his way here was no accident? That he had been guided by some latent memory?

He got up suddenly, and slipping out of the ill-fitting jacket, he opened the closet and took down one of the coats, a city man's black broadcloth coat, excellently tailored. He slipped it on . . . a perfect fit!

The clothes were his, the house was his. He had the deed in his pocket. But obviously the cabin had been occupied by Ruble Noon before the deed was made out . . . no doubt it came to him as part payment for what he was to do, or as an outright gift.

Suppose then that Tom Davidge had been the "Nebraska" cattleman who originally hired him? No . . . the Pinkerton report said that cattleman had been a friend to Tom Davidge.

Davidge had permitted outlaws to stop on his land before, so why not Ruble Noon?

Four men . . . he had taken money to kill four men.

He got up and walked to the window and looked outside. Sunlight fell through the pines and the rawboned ridges were starkly beautiful. In this place there was only the wind, and sometimes the rain, the snow, and the cold. Here change came slowly; a rock crumbled, a tree grew, a root pushed deeper into a crevice, forcing wide the jaws of rock. Here there was only one problem, the problem of existence alone. Down there in the valleys where men walked there were many problems.

He went over to the bookshelves and looked at the titles: Locke's *Essay Concerning Human Understanding*, Mills's *On Liberty*, Blackstone's *Commentaries* on the law, and dozens of others. Could the man who read such books kill for hire? If so, what had happened to him?

The Pinkerton report had accounted in general outline for six years of his life, but what of the time before that? What of the time before he arrived in that Missouri town and went to work for a tie-cutting camp? If he was a mystery to others, he was even more of a mystery to himself.

Ben Janish, now . . . Ben had tried to kill him, and he had apparently taken payment to kill Ben, but he felt no desire to kill him, or anyone else.

Was that why Ben Janish had tried to kill him—because he knew he was a hunted man? Or had he himself tried to kill Janish and failed, and been shot in return?

He knew what he had to do. He must go back, search out his past; he must find out who and what he was. He would go to El Paso. He had the address of Dean Cullane.

He went to the closet again and carefully went through the pockets of every garment. There were no letters, no papers, no addresses . . . nothing.

The desk next. Again failure. There was a quantity of writing paper, there was ink, and there were pens, and there was an account book with a list of figures in it, apparently sums of money running into several thousands, but there was no clue unless it was the initials after several of the sums.

Suddenly he thought of the mirror . . . he had not looked in a mirror since he had become "Jonas," and he had no idea what he looked like.

The face he saw was strange. It was a rather triangular face, with strong cheekbones and a strong jaw. It was a handsome face, in a rugged way. He studied it critically, but saw nothing there that reminded him of anyone or anything.

His eyes went to the patch of bandage on his skull, which needed changing. He removed it, and then, after getting a fire started, he heated water and bathed the wound with care."

He went back to the mirror. There was an older scar there, evidently from a severe blow on the skull. The present cut had glanced across a corner of it, ripping his scalp.

He searched about, found a small drawer of medical supplies, and bandaged the wound again. It was healing fast, and a bandage would soon not be needed. A bandage attracts attention, and he hoped he could do without it before he reached El Paso.

Finding a carpetbag in the closet, he packed a suit, several shirts, and a few other necessary items; then he went out to the stable, stripped the gear from the dun, and turned it loose.

At the mirror he trimmed the several days' growth of beard, and sat down and shined the boots he was wearing. From some storehouse of memory he remembered something: "If you want the law to leave you alone, keep your hair trimmed and your boots shined." There was something to it.

After this he entered the closet, closed the door behind him, and went to the shaft. The arrangement of block and tackle had been done by an expert, and would have handled several times his weight. Taking the bag, he lowered himself down the shaft, taking it easy.

Once men had climbed part way up here ... he could see where steps, now almost obliterated, had been carved into the sandstone. They stopped at a shelf that showed a black cave beyond. Sometime he would take the time to examine that cave.

At the bottom of the shaft he took time to listen, then stepped out. He was in a large, roomy cave. At the front was part of a ruined wall, and he had to walk around fallen rock to reach the outer cave, which was formed merely by an overhang hollowed by wind and rain.

Beyond this a steep path led diagonally down to a sheer cliff that dropped some twenty feet. He looked around and saw a notched pole tucked into a crevice. He took it out, descended by this means, and hid the pole in the brush. From below he could see nothing of the path, only the roof of the overhang.

He looked all around carefully. He saw a trail, an ancient one by the look of it, that led away along the

face of the rock and angled down the slope. There were
no tracks on the trail.

He went slowly, stepping on rocks where he could,
avoiding making any sign of passage. Suddenly he
paused. Around a corner of rock he saw a cabin built
of native stone, with a pole corral, some chickens, and
a few guinea hens. In the corral were several horses and
three cows.

He went up to the cabin, walking warily. An old
Mexican came out and went to the corral. Taking down
a rope, he caught a horse and led it outside.

He spoke to the Mexican, who merely lifed a hand,
and then went to the cabin and returned with a saddle
and the rest of the rigging.

In his own mind he was now quite sure that he was
Ruble Noon. He said, "Has anyone been around?"

The Mexican shook his head. His eyes went to the
bandage, just visible under Noon's hat, but he said
nothing. He was an old man, square and solid, a mus-
cular man with a seamed and scarred face.

Noon touched the bandage. "Dry-gulch," he said, "I
was lucky."

The Mexican shrugged, then gestured toward the
house and made a motion of eating. When his mouth
opened, Ruble Noon saw the man had no tongue.

Noon shook his head, and believing the saddled
horse was for him, he went to it and gathered the reins.
The horse nickered softly, seeming to know him.

"I'll be back in about a week," he said, and the old
Mexican nodded.

The trail dipped down, went through a notch in the
cliffs, and headed southeast. At first, he saw no tracks
on the trail, then a few, obviously many days old. After
an hour's ride he saw something gleaming in the sun,
still some distance off . . . it was the railroad.

He continued on the trail and suddenly found it was
parallel to the railroad and perhaps a mile away from
it. There were rocks and brush at that point, but a

space behind them was beaten by the hoofs of horses, or of one horse tethered there many times. It was a perfect observation point, where a man could wait unseen, watching the railroad and the station.

The station was simply a freight car without wheels, with a chimney made of stovepipe, and a signal for stopping trains.

After watching for several minutes he decided that the place was deserted, and he rode on again along the trail. It wound among a maze of huge boulders, with several other trails coming in to join it, and then it pointed toward the tracks and the station.

The door of the station was on the latch. He opened it, and stepped inside. There was a pot-bellied stove, a woodbox, a bench, and a few faded magazines. He went back outside and raised the stop signal, and settled down to wait.

The fly-speckled schedule told him the train would be along in two hours—a freight train.

All was quiet. Somewhere out on the flat he heard a bird call, but there was no other sound. He looked off across the flat country toward the farthest mountains.

Soon he might know. Somewhere there would be a clue. If he was Ruble Noon now, he might always have been Ruble Noon—but what if he had been somebody else before that? What *was* he? *Who* was he?

In the distance he heard the train. He could hear the rails humming.

Chapter Seven

The train came in sight, whistled, and rolled down the track, the drivers pounding. It consisted of a locomotive, two freight cars, three stock cars, and a caboose.

The brakeman swung down. "Climb aboard," he said. "We're runnin' behind time."

"How about my horse?"

He gave a look at the roan, then indicated an empty stock car. "Load 'im up, but get a move on."

An improvised ramp, three planks nailed together, lay against the building. Noon took one end, the brakeman the other, and they placed it in position. The horse went into the stock car, and in a matter of minutes they were rolling.

Back in the caboose the brakeman went to the stove and took up the coffeepot. "How about it?" he said.

"Sure," Noon said.

The railroader handed him a cup. The coffee was hot, black as midnight, and strong.

"Can't figure you out," the brakeman said. "I've made this run fifty times, maybe, an' nobody ever gets on at that stop but you."

"It's a lonely country."

"Yeah ... it is that. But there's a lot of lonely country, and you're the on'y one I know with your own railroad station."

Noon shrugged. "I'm not complaining. Saves time."

The brakeman finished his coffee and went out to check the train. Ruble Noon put down his cup and stretched out on the settee.

Some hours later he was awakened by the brakeman. "You hungry? We're makin' a stop up ahead. The grub's pretty good."

"Thanks."

It was night. He heard the train's long whistle, looked ahead, and saw the finger of light from the locomotive pushing its way through the darkness. Behind it was the red glow from the firebox. The long whistle sounded again, calling into the night.

He sat for some time in the window, looking into the darkness. Then he saw the lights of a town ahead, a fair-sized town. He took out his watch—it was just past eleven o'clock.

The train ground to a halt. "We'll be here about twenty minutes," the brakeman said. "Don't get too far away."

Noon swung down, following the brakeman, and walked to the station. There was a lunchroom there, and several men were already eating at the long table. Two men who appeared to be cowhands were standing at the bar nursing their beers

As the brakeman entered they turned, glancing from the brakeman to Noon. One of the cowhands said something in a low tone to the man beside him, who gave a sharper look.

Ruble Noon sat down, helped himself to a piece of overdone steak and some mashed potatoes, and started to eat. He was, he discovered, very hungry.

The brakeman spoke out of the side of his mouth. "I don't know you, mister, but it looks like you've got trouble."

Noon was listening, but he did not look up. "All right," he said, and then added, "keep out of it. Let me handle it."

"There's two of 'em," the brakeman protested, "and I ain't had a good fight in months."

"Well," Noon said, "if they use their fists. But if it's guns, leave it to me."

He could hear the low talk at the bar. One man was protesting to the other, but the first was having none of it. Suddenly, he spoke aloud. "You over there! You with the blue coat! Don't I know you from somewhere?"

"You might." Ruble Noon spoke easily. "I've been there."

The man was just drunk enough not to understand. "You been where?" he demanded.

"There," Ruble Noon said gently.

For a moment there was silence, and in the silence somebody chuckled. The man at the bar grew irritated. "I know you from somewhere," he insisted.

"I don't think you know me," Ruble Noon said. He finished his coffee and got to his feet. "If you did you'd keep your mouth shut."

He stepped outside and the brakeman followed, glancing over his shoulder. "I think they're comin out," he said. "They ain't goin' to leave it lay."

"Let's get aboard."

"You scared?"

Ruble Noon turned his head sharply to look at the brakeman. "No, I'm not scared, but I have too much sense to get into a shooting match with a couple of half-drunken cowhands over nothing."

At that moment the train whistled.

Ruble Noon walked along, caught the handrail, and swung up to the step. The two cowhands had emerged from the restaurant and were staring after him. The brakeman hesitated, then swung aboard, completing a hasty signal with his lantern.

One of the cowhands started after them. "Hey, you! You can't get away with that! You—"

Ruble Noon went inside, followed by the brakeman,

who gave him a surly look. "What did you mean back there? I mean when you said if he knew who you were he'd keep his mouth shut?"

"I was just talking."

"I thought so," the brakeman said. But he seemed unsure, and kept staring at Noon. "I don't get this," he said at last. "There's somethin' here I just don't get."

"Forget it," Ruble Noon stretched out on the settee. "Call me before we get to El Paso."

"It'll be daylight." The brakeman hesitated. "You gettin' off at the same place? This side of town?"

"Naturally," Noon said, and closed his eyes. He heard the brakeman leave to go about his business, and after a while he fell asleep.

The siding where they let him off was in a thick growth of brush and trees near a deserted ranch on the outskirts of town.

When he had unloaded his horse at the chute, he watched the train pull away. The brakeman was staring after him, obviously puzzled.

Ruble Noon himself was puzzled. Apparently he had made this trip before and was known to the trainmen, but they did not know his business nor why he should be accorded such privilege. Undoubtedly there was some official connection. Perhaps some of his "work" had been for the railroad. It would take somebody with considerable authority to arrange such a situation.

There was nobody around the small adobe. He saw a well, lowered a bucket, and got water for himself and his horse.

The door of the adobe was closed, but it opened under his hand. The place was dusty, but otherwise it was clean and in good shape. There was a bed, and a cupboard devoid of supplies. It was cool and quiet, and was hidden by mesquite thickets and a few cottonwoods.

He went outside again, and noticed a couple of stacks of hay near the corral. He put some down for the roan, and squatted on his heels in the shade, considering the situation. It would be better, he decided, to wait until dark before entering the town.

As he sat there he found himself thinking back to the two cowhands at the restaurant near the station where they had stopped. For the first time he thought about the one who had tried to avoid trouble. That one, he decided, had not been drinking. Moreover, there had been something peculiar in his attitude, some particular caution. Was he imagining it, or had that cowhand been overeager to avoid trouble?

Was it mere chance that they were there? Suppose one of them was there for a purpose, and the other had just joined him by accident? Suppose one was a spy, an outpost, as it were, to notify somebody of Noon's approach to El Paso?

He was imagining things. Knowing nothing for sure, he was finding suspicious items everywhere.

But the one man's attitude, the way he had looked at Ruble Noon, would not leave him. That man had known who he was looking at, but he had not wanted to attract attention.

All right ... take it from there. Suppose that somebody in El Paso had discovered that Ruble Noon used that approach. Suppose that somebody had a man posted to watch for him at the logical place—the restaurant and bar where all train crews stopped.

The one who wanted such information might be one of two types. He might be somebody who wanted to hire him for a job, or somebody who wanted him killed ... who, for one reason or another, feared him.

If they knew about this route into the town, they might also know about this place. He might, even now, be right in the middle of a trap.

He sat very still, his hatbrim pulled low. Under it his

eyes were busy, searching out places of possible concealment.

The pile of wood yonder . . . possible, but unlikely—too hard to get at or get away from. Under the mesquite? His eyes searched that spot, and suddenly all his senses were alert. Was some sixth sense, or perhaps all his other senses together, trying to warn him of something? Or was it only his imagination that made him suspect he might be under observation?

Were they waiting for him to move? If so, why? If they wanted to kill him, why hadn't they tried it already

He went over his every move. He had approached under cover of the brush and trees; he had been only momentarily in the open when he fed the horse and when he went into the house.

If somebody was waiting here, that somebody was waiting for him to do some expected thing he had not yet done. He evidently had not put himself in the line of fire yet; but why didn't the man move into a different position? If he had not done so, it must be because he could not without attracting attention. Which indicated that the unseen man, if there was one, was in a position where he would draw attention to himself if he moved. It would, no doubt, be a position with an easy escape route, in case his shot was a miss.

Suppose he himself had arrived at this place with a memory that was not confused? What would he have done? As there were no supplies in the adobe, and no sign of occupancy, it was likely he would have ridden away. No doubt that was exactly what he had done in the past. If the marksman believed that to be the case, where would he be? Obviously, somewhere along the road that led away from the ranch, in some place that did not allow him to cover the ranch yard itself.

Was he imagining all this? Or was there actually someone hidden nearby, someone primed and ready to kill?

If there was a man waiting, he must be growing nervous and restless by now. It might be that he could be provoked into a move. But on the other hand, he might have the patience of an Indian and lie quiet, knowing that Noon must sooner or later leave the place.

He got up and went into the adobe, and crossed to the back room. He did not want to kill anyone, but neither did he want to be killed. He looked out the back window.

A dozen yards away there was a ditch masked by undergrowth. He studied it for a long moment. It looked inviting, too inviting. Glancing around, he saw a large olla such as the Mexicans use to cool water. On the bed lay an old blanket. He took it up, wrapped it around the olla, put his hat over the top, and thrust it up to the window. It looked like a man about to climb through. A rifleman, tense with waiting, might—

The olla had not been in position an instant when there was the crash of a volley . . . more than two rifles . . . three, at least. The olla shattered under his hand.

He raced for the front of the adobe and was in time to see a man running from behind the stable toward Noon's horse. If they got his horse he was trapped . . . to be killed at leisure.

He never knew when he drew. The sight of the running man, the realization of what this meant, and his own draw must have been simultaneous. He heard the bellow of his gun in the close confines of the room as he shot through the open door.

The runner took two steps, then stumbled and hit the ground. And then silence. . . .

The bare, hard-packed earth of the yard was empty, except for the dead man and the horse. Nervously, the roan had moved nearer.

Keeping his voice low, Ruble Noon called to the horse, which looked toward him uncertainly.

A boot grated on gravel behind the adobe. They

were coming for him. The roan was nearer now, no more than fifteen or twenty feet off. The long stable was a wall between the yard and the thickets beyond. There were at least three men out behind, and they were hunting him now. He could try for the horse. . . .

Suddenly he knew he was not going to run. Not yet. They had planned for that, were ready for it. He backed into a corner where he could watch the door and the windows at the same time.

He thumbed back the loading gate of his Colt and thrust out the empty shell, then added a fresh cartridge. Moving the cylinder, he added another. The six-shooter was now fully loaded.

He could see a shadow at the window. Somebody was looking into the room, but the corner where Noon stood could not be seen.

Someone else was at the door. Would they be so foolish as to try a rush?

"Now!"

The word came sharply, and three men leaped into the room, two through windows, one from the door. It was their first mistake.

They came out of the bright sunlight into the dim light of the room, and one man stumbled as he landed from the window. All held guns, but only one got off a shot. He fired as he was falling, the gun blasting its bullet into the floor.

Ruble Noon shot as they came, and held the gun in his hand and waited a slow minute while he watched the windows and the door. One of the men on the floor stirred and moaned. Noon squatted on his heels and stayed quiet.

Outside nothing stirred, and then he heard a magpie. Following that he heard the pound of hoofs racing away . . . one rider.

They had thought to surprise him, not thinking of the dimness inside, and he was in the darkest corner, the last place on which their eyes could focus.

Now the wounded man was staring at him through wide, pain-filled eyes. "You goin' to shoot me?" he asked.

"No."

"They said you was a killer."

"Who said so? Who hired you?"

"I ain't goin' to tell you that. They said you was a back-shootin' killer."

"I don't need to shoot men in the back."

"No," the wounded man admitted, "I guess you don't. . . . But there's one still out there."

"No. He rode away—I heard him." Ruble Noon was thinking hard. He said, "What will he do? Will he bring others?"

"Him?" The wounded man spoke bitterly. "That there louse? He'll run his hoss's legs off gittin' away. Never was no fight in him!"

Ruble Noon holstered his gun and moved over to the wounded man. He had hit twice, once through the shoulder, the second time through the leg. Working as swiftly as he could, Noon plugged the wounds and wrapped them with bandages torn from a dead man's shirt.

"Where'd you leave your horse?" he asked.

The man stared at him. "You goin' to run me out of here?"

"I'm going to get you out of here. Or do you want to explain those?" He gestured to the dead men. "You came here to murder me . . . remember?"

"We sure didn't cut the mustard," the man said. "You outfoxed us."

Noon collected the guns from the dead men, and packed them outside. He collected their horses and tied the dead men on them. He pinned on each one a paper which read:

He tried to dry-gulch
Ruble Noon

Then he turned the horses loose.

The wounded man raised up on an elbow. "What was them papers you pinned on them?"

"It makes no difference," Noon answered, and sat down. "Now you and I are going to have a little talk."

The gunman looked at him warily. He was a grizzled, hard-faced man with a broken nose. "About what?"

"About who hired you."

"An' supposin' I ain't of a mind to?"

Ruble Noon shrugged. "I'll just pull out those plugs I put in you and I won't tell anybody where you are. You might manage to walk a mile, but I doubt it. You'd start bleeding again and before dark you'd be buzzard meat."

The gunman lay back and closed his eyes. "Mister, I don't know who it was. These boys an' me was in a joint ... the Acme Saloon, it was. There was a gent come in we knew as Peterson. It wasn't his real name, but that's of no matter. Anyway, he said we could pick up fifty dollars apiece and he wanted five of us, for a little shooting.

"He said this was a known man, and there'd be no worry about the law if we done it. This here Peterson had been in the Rangers at one time, and he knowed a lot of folks around about town. We taken his word for it. We'd seen him talkin' with some high-powered men around El Paso, like A. J. Fountain, the Mannings, Magoffin, and the like of that.

"He laid it out for us, but all the time we knowed he was talkin' for somebody else and not for himself. You see, this Peterson knowed a lot of folks on both sides of the fence, and he'd been a sort of go-between before this. If a man wanted to sell stolen cattle, Peterson could always put him in the way of it.

"Fifty dollars now, that's near two months' wages for a cowhand, so we taken him up on it. Who paid the money to him, I don't know."

Ruble Noon considered. The man seemed to be telling the truth, and the story sounded right.

"All right," he said. "I've got your horse outside. I'm going to load you up and take you out a ways. When I get you within easy distance of El Paso I'll turn you loose."

He stood for a moment thinking about Peterson. It was unlikely that he could make Peterson talk, for the man sounded like a tough one. He had served in the Rangers, and had probably gone bad after leaving them . . . or been kicked out, as was often the case if they found they had a bad egg in the basket.

When those dead men came into town tied on their horses, Peterson would be among the first to hear of it, and he would surely carry the news to the man who had hired him. By watching Peterson, Ruble Noon might locate his man.

Now he loaded the wounded man on his horse and led the animal away from the deserted ranch. When they were well on the road to El Paso, he let the horse and rider go.

He swung off the trail into the mesquite and circled for low ground, riding toward El Paso by the best hidden route he could find.

Had he been here before? It seemed likely that he had. Should he let himself go, hoping that hidden memory would take him to the right places?

But those places might now be the worst ones for him, and any man he saw might be an enemy. Or he might be wanted by the law.

He rode on cautiously, but with foreboding. His head was aching again, and he was very tired. The sun was hot, and he wanted to lie down in the shade to rest, but there was no time.

He was riding toward something, he did not know what. The only thing he was sure of now was that he was Ruble Noon, a man feared, a man who hired his gun to kill, a man he did not want to be.

Whatever had made him what he was he did not know; he knew only that he wanted to be that no longer. The trouble was, he had to be. To cease to be what he was now would be to die ... and to leave that girl back there alone, and without defenses.

He rode on in the hot afternoon, and the streets of the town opened before him.

Chapter Eight

As he entered the town a street on his right branched away from the main street, and he turned into it. When he had ridden only a few hundred yards he saw a large wooden stable with doors opened wide. An old Mexican sat in front of it. There were a water trough and a pump close by.

He drew up. "You got room for another horse?" he asked.

The Mexican looked at him. "This is not a livery stable, señor," he said, "but if you wish—"

Ruble Noon swung to the ground. "It's the first one I saw," he said, "and I'm dead beat. How much for the horse and a place to clean up?"

"Fifty cents?"

"That'll do." He followed the Mexican into the stable and was shown a stall. He led the roan in, then went up to the loft and forked hay down the chute into the manger.

When he came down he gave the Mexican fifty cents, and followed him to the water trough. The Mexican handed him a tin basin, and he pumped water into it and washed his face and hands, and then combed his hair. Using his hat, he whipped the dust from his pants and his boots.

When he turned to go the old man said, "You wish to sleep here, señor? There is a cot in there." He gestured toward a room in the corner of the barn. "And no bugs."

"How much?"

The Mexican smiled. "Fifty cents."

"All right."

He turned to walk away and the man spoke again. "Be careful, señor."

He stopped, his eyes searching the old man's face. "Why do you say that?"

The man shrugged. "It is a wild town. The railroads have brought many strangers. There have been shootings."

"Thanks," Noon said.

The sun had slipped from sight, and with its passing a desert coolness came. He walked to the next street, and saw the sign of the Coliseum, a saloon and variety theater. He avoided it ... from somewhere he seemed to have the impression that the Coliseum and Jack Doyle's were the most popular places in town.

In a small restaurant further along the street he ordered *frijoles, tortillas,* and roast beef, and drank a glass of beer. Over his coffee he sat watching the lights come on. Men came and went as he waited there. Having eaten, he felt better, and the ache dulled, but he was strangely on edge, not at all as he wanted to feel.

He got up to pay, and a small man eating at a table near him turned suddenly to look at him ... and stared.

Ruble Noon paid his bill and went outside, but he felt uneasy. When he had walked a few yards he glanced back, and saw that the man was standing in the restaurant door, staring after him.

He turned the corner, walked a block, and crossed the street. Glancing back he saw no one, but he felt worried. That man was interested in him, and recognized him perhaps. The sooner he did what he had come to do and left town, the better.

He saw the Acme Saloon ahead of him ... and then

he saw the sign of Dean Cullane's office. It was on the second floor, reached by an outside stairway. The windows were dark and the place was empty-looking.

He paused and made a show of wiping his face while he glanced up and down the street. No one was in sight, and he went up the steps swiftly. At the landing he knocked, and when there was no response he tried the door. It was locked.

He looked down, but there was no one on the street. He drew his knife, slipped the point into the lock, and worked the bolt back, then he pushed with his shoulder. The door was ill-fitting, and it opened easily. He stepped inside and pushed it to behind him.

He stood still . . . listening.

Outside there was only the distant tin-panny sound of a piano. He waited, letting his eyes grow accustomed to the dim light that came in through the windows.

He saw that the room contained a rolltop desk, a swivel chair, another chair, and a leather settee. Under a shelf filled with books there was also a table covered with papers. A brass spittoon was on the floor.

A door stood open just a crack, and in that crack he saw a gun muzzle. Even as he saw it, he realized that the something that had disturbed him since entering the room was the faint smell of perfume mingled with the smell of stale tobacco.

"There's no use of your shooting me," he said. "There would be nothing gained. And besides"—he played a hunch—"you'd have to explain what you were doing here."

The door opened wider, and he could see a girl standing there, the gun still held level. "Who are you?" she asked.

He smiled into the darkness, and some of the smile was in his tone when he said, "I didn't ask you that."

"All right then—what do you want?"

"To put some pieces together."

"What was Dean Cullane to you?" she asked.

"A name—no more than that. Only somebody shot at me, and a thing like that makes a man curious."

"Dean Cullane would not shoot anyone—at least, I don't think he would."

"We never know, do we? Sometimes the most unexpected people will shoot. You even have a gun yourself."

"But I would shoot, mister. I have shot before this."

"And killed?"

"I didn't have time to look. Anyway, Dean Cullane did not shoot you, so who did? And why are you here?"

"The man who shot at me was paid to do it. He is a man who does such things for money."

"Ruble Noon!" she exclaimed.

"Is he the only one? I have heard there are a dozen here in El Paso, or over in Juarez, who would kill for hire."

By now he realized that she was young and appeared to be attractive, and she was well gotten up, but not for the street ... at least not for El Paso streets at this hour. And not for the vicinity of the Acme Saloon at any hour.

"Whatever you are here for," the girl said, "you have no business to be in this office. You forced the door."

"And you had a key? Perhaps Dean Cullane had a reason to give you a key."

"He did not give it to me, and it does not mean what you think. Dean Cullane was my brother."

"Was?"

"He is dead ... he was killed ... murdered."

"I am sorry. I didn't know that. If you are his sister you have a right to be here." He reached toward the kerosene lamp. "Shall we have some light?"

"No! Please don't! He would kill me, too."

"Who?"

"Ruble Noon ... the man who killed Dean."

He held himself very still, listening for something

within him, but nothing spoke to him. . . . Had he actually killed Dean Cullane?

"I doubt if he would kill a woman," he said. "It isn't done, you know."

He removed the lamp chimney, struck a match, and held it to the wick. As he did so, she lowered the gun, and when he replaced the chimney, they looked across the room at each other.

He saw a slender girl, with auburn hair and dark eyes; at least, in this light they seemed to be dark. She was dressed for a party, but had a dark cloak over her arm. She was lovely . . . a real beauty.

Her eyes fell to his sleeve. "Where did you get that coat?" Her voice was suddenly cold. "That is my brother's coat, Dean's coat. I was with him when he chose the material."

"It is? All I knew was that it was not mine. I must have taken it by mistake."

"You don't know?"

"No." He touched his head. "I was struck on the head. I believe I tried to escape from somewhere after I was struck, and I must have caught up a coat from where mine was hanging."

"Where was this?"

"Northwest of here . . . quite a way off. . . . You spoke of Ruble Noon. Did your brother know him?"

"No, but he was trying to discover who he was, what he was. I do not know why, but I believe Dean had some information that related to Ruble Noon in some way. He told me he had to see him, to talk to him, and he seemed to think he knew where to find him."

"You are dressed for a party?" he said inquiringly.

"Yes. I came from one at the home of friends, and I must get back." But she made no move to go. She was giving him all her attention. "What are you going to do?" she asked.

"Stay here and look."

"For what?"

"Ma'am, somebody shot at me. Before they try it again I want to know why they're shooting. I picked up Dean Cullane's coat in the room where I got shot at, or somewhere close by. Dean Cullane is my only clue . . . except one other."

"What is that?"

"I know who shot at me." He paused. "Miss Cullane, what do you know about the Rafter D—Tom Davidge's outfit?"

She hesitated before replying. That she knew something was obvious, and apparently she was wondering whether to tell him of it or not. "I know nothing about the ranch," she said finally. "I did know Fan, Tom Davidge's daughter. We went to school together."

He was getting nowhere. And he did not have much time, for without doubt the people who had sent men gunning for him knew he was in El Paso. They would also have an idea of where to look for him.

As he talked his eyes had been taking in the room, locating possible hiding places for whatever it was that he wanted.

"We must go," she said suddenly. "They will be wondering where I am."

"I'll stay," he said.

She smiled at him. "Of course, I cannot demand that you accompany me, but would a gentleman allow a lady to walk the streets of El Paso alone at this hour?"

He shrugged. "I hope I am a gentleman, ma'am, but I have a distinct impression that you got here by yourself . . . and you are armed."

Her eyes narrowed a little as the skin tightened around them. This young lady had a temper—and she was used to having her own way.

"If you stay here," she said, "I shall have you arrested. You broke in here, like a thief. I suspect you are a thief."

He had an idea she meant what she said, and he responded, "All right. I will walk you back to the party."

He took her key to lock the door, but she held out her hand for it and he had to return it. They went down the steps and along the street, then around a corner and down another street. He could hear the music and laughter before they saw the house.

It was a white frame house with a lot of gingerbread decorations around the eaves. He went to the steps with her and stopped, about to turn away.

"Peg? Peg Cullane! Who's that with you?"

A girl came down the steps. She was shorter than Peg Cullane, and was blonde and pretty and plump. She looked up at him and laughed.

"Leave it to Peg! She's the only girl in town who could step out for a breath of fresh air and come back with the handsomest man in town! ... Well? Are you coming in?"

"Sorry," Ruble Noon said. "I have to be going. I was just walking Miss Cullane back to the dance."

"Oh, no, you don't! Not without at least one dance with me. Peg, aren't you going to introduce me?"

"My name is Mandrin," he said, "Jonas Mandrin."

"And I am Stella Mackay ... just Stella to you! Let's all go in."

A gray-haired man was standing outside on the lawn smoking a cigar. Ruble Noon saw him look up quickly when he said he was Jonas Mandrin ... and then look again sharply.

Mandrin? It was another of those names that had come from nowhere, involuntarily. Jonas Mandrin ... it was not a usual name—like Tom Jones or John Smith, not the sort of name a man might be expected to come up with suddenly. He might, without meaning to at all, be giving a clue to his identity.

The music was playing, and he found himself inside dancing with Stella, but he watched Peg Cullane. She was not dancing. He saw her go across the room to a tall young man and speak to him. At once the man's eyes sought him out, and then the man went to two others in the room, and all stood together, watching him.

Trouble ... he would be a fool not to see it coming. Stella was talking gaily, and he was replying. ... What was he doing here, she was asking. He heard himself saying he was looking for ranch property, wanting to raise horses.

He finished the dance with Stella, danced with another girl, and had stopped briefly at one side of the room. The man he had seen smoking on the lawn came up and spoke to him quietly. He was a fine-looking elderly man, with clean-cut features and a scholarly face.

"Young man," he said, "if you want to live out the evening you had better slip away." He paused for a moment. "The gate at the end of the garden is open. Go through it to the house next door. The side door. On the other side of the house the side door is open. Go in and sit down in that room, but do not make a light."

"Is that a trap?"

The old man smiled. "No, Jonas Mandrin, it is not. It is my home, and I am Judge Niland. You will be safe in my house." All this had been in a low tone.

The music started again, and he danced around the room through the crowd. When near the door to the kitchen, and opposite the three young men, he whispered a quick good-bye to the girl with whom he was dancing and slipped out through the kitchen. Then he was running.

It was dark outside. He did not open the gate, but touched a hand lightly on the top and vaulted. He landed and, skirting a huge cottonwood, found himself in the Judge's yard. He went to the door on the other side and it opened under his hand and he stepped into the darkness of the room.

The air was close; the room was still except for the ticking of the clock. Only faintly could he hear music from the house he had left. He touched a chair, and sat down.

A moment later he heard running feet, and the sound of somebody swearing. Standing up, he leaned over and flipped the lock on the door.

He heard the steps come close, and a hand trying the door. Then someone said, low-voiced, "Not there, you fool! That's the Judge's house!" And then they were gone.

He eased back into the chair, slowly relaxing. His forehead was damp with perspiration, and he felt tired. He was still weak from that blow on the head and from the loss of blood.

Gradually his tenseness slackened, and presently he fell asleep.

Chapter Nine

He awoke suddenly, to find himself slouched down in the chair. The room was still in darkness, but there was light from an open door down a hallway. He got to his feet, listening.

In that lighted room he could hear the scratching of a pen. He went down the hall and stopped by the door.

Judge Niland sat at a table writing. He glanced up and gestured toward a chair. "Have a seat. I'll be with you in a moment," he said.

When he had finished what he was writing and had blotted the paper, he took off his glasses and put his hands on the table.

"I suppose you are wondering why I have done this," he said, "and just where I fit into this picture."

"Yes."

"I heard you introduce yourself as Jonas Mandrin, and was surprised. But after a few minutes' thought I knew I shouldn't be at all surprised—except that you are alive."

"You have told me nothing."

"No, I suppose not. Then accept this as truth. I am your friend, and I should like to continue to be your friend. I also, it might be said, was a friend to Tom Davidge."

"Then tell me: Why should Peg Cullane put those men on me?"

77

Judge Niland was surprised now. He threw a sharp glance at Noon, and said, "But you should understand that. Peg is money-hungry, and she wants that money. She was the one who egged Dean into making his try for it. They are afraid of you because they are sure you know where it is."

Money? What money?

"They could be wrong," he said.

"Yes, but even if they are wrong, they know you were sent here to get rid of Ben Janish. . . . Oh, yes! I know who you are! That was why you surprised me when you said you were Jonas Mandrin."

"Did you expect me to introduce myself as Ruble Noon?"

"Of course not. What I cannot understand is how Ruble Noon could use the name Jonas Mandrin. Unless—"

"Yes?"

"Unless Ruble Noon and Jonas Mandrin were somehow connected."

Ruble Noon offered no comment. He had no idea who Jonas Mandrin was, but he was very curious as to how Judge Niland knew he was Ruble Noon.

The Judge was obviously a man of property and of importance. The house which they were in gave evidence of luxury. It was more like an eastern house than a western house at this period. The furnishings of the East were expensive items west of the Mississippi, and the cost of transporting them was high. The walls of this house were lined with books, and not all of them were the Judge's law library.

"I was Tom Davidge's attorney," Judge Niland said. "I am still his daugher's attorney. I knew when he began liquidating his eastern holdings, and I knew why he did it. I wrote his will. I also took steps to eliminate Janish and his outfit. Those steps were failures.

"I am afraid that Tom was a believer in somewhat more violent methods than I would lend myself to.

When my way failed—I had gone to the law—he hired you.

"Tom never told me how he got in touch with you, or what he knew about you. All he would say was that he knew the man for the job. Had he been younger I do believe he would have tried it himself.

"The trouble seems to have been that he made arrangements for you to be paid by the worst man possible under the circumstances. You see, Tom Davidge never realized that anyone else knew of what he was doing with his money. We may never know how Peg Cullane found out, but she did. She thought she knew where the money was, but she was sure that you had been told that, too. And so you had to be killed before you could recover it . . . either for Fan or for yourself."

"So she told Ben Janish who I was, and why I was coming out there?"

"No, she didn't. She had her brother do it. Dean pulled out of here suddenly after Tom died, and he hasn't been seen since. Just the other day we received a report that he was dead."

"And that I had killed him?"

"Something like that." Niland looked at him inquiringly. "Did you?"

"No." Even as he said it, he knew he really didn't know. But he did not believe he had, or did not want to believe it.

"You were accused of it."

Did that explain the mob at the station? The men who searched the train?

"If you have not grasped the situation," Judge Niland said slowly, "you must. Fan Davidge does not even know there is half a million dollars hidden on her ranch. She does not know there is any money at all.

"Dean Cullane knew, but he is dead. Peg Cullane knows, but she is not going to tell Fan. She wants that money for herself. And Peg does not know that I know, although she has probably wondered about it.

She would assume that if I knew I would tell Fan, but I haven't done so, and she knows I have not."

"How about Ben Janish?"

"A good question." Judge Niland sat back in his chair and put the tips of his fingers together. "And if you did not kill Dean Cullane, who did? If it was Ben Janish who killed Dean, then Ben must know about the money. I can think of no other reason why he would kill him."

"Then," Ruble Noon commented thoughtfully, "if Ben Janish knows, and you and I know . . ."

The Judge smiled slightly. "It seems we have to get rid of Ben—and quickly."

"Could Dean Cullane have known where the money was?"

"No." Judge Niland was firm. "Tom Davidge knew just what sort of man Dean was. Dean came of a good family, but he was a jackleg lawyer, and one who dealt with men on the wrong side of the law in ways not concerned with the legal profession. Davidge might use Dean to act as a go-between to cover his own trail, but he would never confide in him. That, of course, does not rule out that Dean might know Davidge had the money."

Ruble Noon was silent. Being silent had proved a good way to be, for he had learned almost all he needed to know—almost all.

"Tom Davidge was a shrewd man," Judge Niland went on. "He suffered reverses in the East, though not such bad reverses that he had no money. What he did know, however, was that the wolves would be on his trail; so, as quietly as possible, he turned whatever he could into cash and negotiable securities. Negotiable," he repeated, "but he would use someone who knows how to negotiate them, and who would not be questioned by those with whom he negotiated." He smiled again. "Not a drifting gunman, for instance, or some unknown person from out of nowhere."

Ruble Noon shrugged. "There are 'fences.' There are always men who can handle such things."

"But at great cost, my friend, a far greater cost, let us say, than an even split. With a fence, you'd be lucky to get forty cents on the dollar. On the other hand, you could have sixty—with forty for your partner."

So there it was . . . out in the open.

Or was it? Suppose the Judge was merely testing him?

"I suppose you could look at it that way," he said, "but there's still Ben Janish."

"A job for which you have already been paid."

"What about Tom Davidge's daughter?"

"She will have the ranch, free and clear. It is all she expects to have."

Then Judge Niland straightened up. "There it is, my friend. Although I am no longer a judge, I do have connections. It would be a simple thing for me to arrange that all charges against you are dropped. I could also handle the securities without trouble."

"And I take care of the obstacle? Of Ben Janish?"

"Exactly. You, and only you, know where the money is hidden. I do not know why Tom Davidge trusted you, but he did. We need each other, you and I."

He was impelled to laugh at the irony of it, but he held his face still. Only he knew where the half-million dollars was hidden, and he had lost his memory! He could just imagine trying to convince the Judge of that.

"It seems the first order of business is Janish," he said; "but what about Peg Cullane?"

Niland looked straight at him. "I was thinking about her," he said. "She could become a problem . . . if she lives."

Ruble Noon kept his eyes down, not to show the anger in him. What manner of man was Ruble Noon if Niland could suggest that he murder a woman? Or was it the Judge's idea that a man who was willing to kill might as easily kill a woman as a man? When he looked up, his face was calm.

"One thing at a time," he said, committing himself to nothing.

He was puzzled at himself, and at the fix he was in. He was wondering if he meant to do what the Judge implied, or seemed to imply.

A half-million—that was more money than he could imagine. It was true that Fan had the ranch, or would have it after he killed Ben Janish ... if he killed him. But that was just it. He could not take the money unless he left her with something, with the ranch. If he killed Ben Janish she would be free—she'd have it then.

But suppose Janish killed *him*? What had happened back there in that nameless town? How had Janish shot at him without his knowing? How had Janish almost killed him?

Of course, he'd been warned. Dean Cullane had warned him.

Well, there was no use his thinking about it; he would not kill Ben Janish. The man who was willing to kill was in another life; now he did not want to kill. Anyway, he did not know where the money was. If he had ever known, he did not know now.

He stood up. "I've got miles to go," he said.

"You'd best be careful. Don't you low-rate that girl. Peg is sly as a fox—I've seen it before this. And she's cold. She'll have her boys out looking for you."

"Who were those men?" Ruble Noon asked.

"Some of the town boys, and some from ranches around," Niland answered. "They set store by her; she's the belle of the country around. Those boys will do anything for her, though some of them are decent enough lads. You be careful now."

Ruble Noon paused at the door. "You going back by trail?" the Judge asked.

Noon shrugged, and did not really answer the question. "There's always the railroad. Tom Davidge owned stock in it, you know. He financed the building of a good part of it, and brought others in to do the rest. And they stood by him, that lot. They'd do anything for old Tom."

He added, "It will take time, Judge. Ben Janish is no fool."

"You bring it here," Niland said. "Right here to me, but come by night. If nobody knows we're acquainted it will help."

When Ruble Noon stepped outside the dark doorway he stood still for a moment, listening. Sometimes it seemed that he had been living in a dream from which he might wake up at any moment. He kept expecting to wake up.

He moved away from the door, but did not go to the gate. Instead, he walked along the hedge to the place where he remembered there was a small gap. Easing through it, he crossed the yard in the darkness, and reached a street. He went on until he came to the stable where he had left his horse.

Not until he was settling down to sleep in the hay did he remember: He had forgotten to get the talk around to Jonas Mandrin.

Who was Jonas Mandrin? How did he fit into the life of Ruble Noon?

Chapter Ten

He awoke to the sound of rain, and for a moment he lay still, listening. Suddenly he heard a low voice calling, calling very softly. "Señor? Señor?"

"*Si?*"

"I think they look for you, señor. It is better you go now."

Ruble Noon stood up and brushed the hay from his clothes, eased his gun into position, and came down the ladder from the loft.

"They have not come here yet," the Mexican said, "but they look on another street. I see them." He had already saddled the roan.

"Is there a way out of here, keeping off the streets?"

The Mexican squatted on his heels and traced in the dust with his finger. "Between the adobes . . . see? Then around the house of Alvarado . . . past the barn and into the brush. I wish you luck, señor."

Ruble Noon led the horse to the back door and stepped into the saddle. The rain was falling harder now.

The Mexican went to the small room and took a poncho from a nail. "Here, take this . . . I will pay. And go with God."

Ruble Noon took a gold eagle from his pocket and handed it to him. "Don't spend it for a few days, *amigo*. They might guess where it came from."

He walked the horse through the door, then cantered along the route the Mexican had indicated. The poncho was merely a thickly woven blanket, with a hole in the center for his head. Wearing the wide-brimmed hat, he might easily pass for a Mexican.

Outside of town he took to the brush. Weaving his way through mesquite thickets, he made for the railroad. The rain fell steadily, and it was likely that whatever trail he left would soon be wiped out. Several times he drew up in the partial shelter of trees to study his back trail, but he saw no one, and of course there was no dust. But visibility was not good, and it made him uneasy.

It was out of the question to return to the ranch after the recent ambush there, so he took a trail northward toward Mesilla. His every instinct was to run and hide, to hole up somewhere and wait until he could sort out his knowledge and his feelings, to come nearer to discovering more about himself.

He must have been a killer, but before that he had been somebody else, somewhere else. Suddenly he thought of newspaper files. If he could go through the files he might find in one of the back issues some report of himself, or some information about Jonas Mandrin. But he must proceed very carefully. He might be known in Mesilla.

It was past nine o'clock when he rode into the quiet town near the Rio Grande. A few lights showed from the doors of saloons, and here and there men were seated on benches or chairs along the boardwalk. One chair was in front of the newspaper office.

He drew up and stepped down from the saddle, and a man seated there looked up curiously.

Ruble Noon knew that this was a time in which to be wary. The Lincoln County war was playing itself out, the warriors were beginning to drift to more healthful climes, but haphazard violence continued. Solitary riders were apt to be regarded with some suspicion until there destinations and intentions became clear.

He looked up the quiet street. He would have liked to sit in one of those chairs himself, listening to the sound of voices, waiting to go to bed until the night had cooled somewhat.

"A pleasant evening," he said. "You're not working?" he asked. He was taking it for granted that the man belonged on the newspaper.

"No. This is a case when no news is good news," the man said. His voice sounded young. "Riding through?"

"As a matter of fact, I was going to ask if I might go over the files of your papers. Last year, maybe, or the year before."

"Now, that's the first time I've been asked that." The newspaper man sat up. "Not many people care what happened that long ago. Anything I can help you with? I've a good memory." He stood at the door of the office.

"Hell, no. To tell you the truth, I was just wanting to get the feel of the country. You know, a man can read a lot between the lines of a newspaper, and I want to see what goes on around."

"Help yourself. Try that set of drawers over there."

"Do you copy much news from out of town? Or much eastern news?"

The man's attention suddenly became sharper. "Ocassionally," he said. "If it has any local connection we do, or if it is of major interest. Once in a while we use eastern or California stuff just to fill in space. Local news usually gets around by grapevine before we can print it."

Ruble Noon went inside and took out the first sheaf of newspapers from the drawer. Settling down near the light, he began to scan the pages.

Outside, the printer turned a little in his chair. His attention had been arrested by the use of the word "copy." It was a newspaperman's use of the word. He had heard it used in this way many times in the East, but rarely west of the Mississippi.

That did not imply that this stranger had been a newspaperman, but he had seen a good many of them drifting along the trails—more since the railroad had come in a few months back. Mallory himself was a tramp printer who had worked on more than a dozen newspapers, and not so much as a year on any of them after his first, when he was fourteen. He had worked in big towns and small ones, but he preferred the little towns, and the western ones.

He had been in Mesilla for only three months now, but he was about ready to drift. He was going to try Santa Fe next, or perhaps go to Arizona. He lighted his pipe and tipped back his chair. This stranger, now ... what he had said was true: the best way to make a quick judgment of a town was through its newspaper, to read the advertisements, the news items on local issues ... but Mallory did not for a minute believe this man was interested in settling in Mesilla.

The fact was that Las Cruces was the coming town. Since the railroad had come to Las Cruces the population here had fallen off a little, and the center of activity seemed to be shifting. For himself, he liked Mesilla.

He stoked his pipe again, and glanced around, hitching his chair a little to watch the stranger, who had finished one sheaf of papers and gone on to another. He was scanning the paper with a rapidity that Mallory envied. He was obviously looking for something particular, and he seemed to be checking most of the items.

The difficulty was that Ruble Noon did not himself know what he was looking for. Some mention of Jonas Mandrin, perhaps, or some news story that might jog his memory, some clue from the time before he was shot. He was trying to eliminate all items that offered no interest, reading more carefully those items that might provide him with the information he wanted.

He was on the fourth sheaf of newspapers and it was almost midnight when he found an item tucked away in a corner of the newspaper.

DISAPPEARANCE

The $500 reward offered for information as to the whereabouts of Jonas Mandrin has been withdrawn, as Mandrin, who disappeared two years ago, is presumed dead.

Mandrin, despondent after the murder of his wife and child during his absence in New York, was reported seen in St. Louis and in Memphis, but then dropped from sight.

A noted hunter of big game and a crack shot, he was president of the newly founded Mandrin Arms Co. of Louisville. He had formerly been a correspondent for various newspapers and magazines in both the United States and Europe.

The discovery of several items of clothing and letters has led to the belief that Jonas Mandrin is dead.

Ruble Noon sat very still, staring at the item. The newspaper he held in his hands was five years old, and Jonas Mandrin had disappeared two years prior to that time. The man known as Ruble Noon had appeared in a Missouri tie-camp about a year after the disappearance. It all seemed to fit nicely.

Was he Jonas Mandrin? If so, what led Jonas Mandrin, a sportsman and businessman, to become Ruble Noon, the mankiller?

He returned the papers to the filing cabinet, and went to the door.

"Find what you wanted?" Mallory asked.

Ruble Noon took off his hat and ran his fingers through his hair. "Well, it seems like a good place," he said, "although the railroad will make a difference."

He stepped into the saddle and started down the street, looking for a livery stable.

Mallory got up and went inside. He took down the first sheaf of papers and leafed through them, checking item after item. But it was not until the next day when he returned to the task that he at last found the item about Jonas Mandrin.

He sat back, considering. The reward had been withdrawn, but there might still be somebody who would pay for information. It was worth a chance.

If not worth five hundred dollars, it might be worth a hundred or more even now. He pulled a sheet of paper across the desk and picked up his pen.

Chapter Eleven

Ruble Noon awoke in his hotel room in the cool hours of morning, and lay on his back staring up at the ceiling. He had the decision clear in his mind that he would return to the Rafter D. Once there, he would face the issues as they developed.

If he had been the man called Jonas Mandrin, he did not know it or feel it. If he had had a wife and child, he had no memory of them. Was his amnesia a curtain to protect him from the destruction that might be wrought by shock and grief?

If he was Jonas Mandrin, had he come west to escape from his memories? Or had he hoped to find the men who had killed his family? If it was the latter case they were safe from him, for he had no details, nothing.

But how had Judge Niland guessed he was Mandrin merely by the use of the name? Or had he known Mandrin at some earlier time, or known of him?

He swung his feet to the floor and dressed quickly, trimmed his beard, and combed his hair. In the dining room he ate a quick breakfast, picked up a lunch he had packed for him, and headed out of town at a fast gallop.

He could have caught the train at Las Cruces, but decided against it. If they were watching the railroad, that would be the logical place. He rode hard, swapped horses at a small ranch, and continued on. The gray he picked up in exchange for the roan was a short-coupled horse with a rough gait, but he was built for stamina.

It was just past sundown when he heard the sound of a cowbell, and topping out on a bluff near the river, he saw a ranch nestled among some cottonwoods on a small creek that ran toward the Rio Grande.

He circled around to the trail down the bluff and rode to the ranch. By the time he reached the place it was dark, but there was a light in the window, which was extinguished when a dog began barking furiously. He drew up and hailed the house, first in English, then in Spanish.

When there was no reply he walked his horse forward into the ranchyard. He stopped there, and called out again.

Someone under the cottonwoods near the house spoke. "What do you wish, señor?"

"A meal, and a horse you'll swap me for this one."

"Where do you go?"

"Socorro, *amigo*."

The Mexican walked out from under the trees. "You may ride up, señor, but my son ... he is under the trees with a Winchester."

"You are wise, *amigo*. Many bad *hombres* ride these days."

He swung down and turned the horse so that they could see him more clearly. "It is a good horse," he said, "but I ride far and I have enemies."

The Mexican shrugged. "A man can be judged by those who hate him. *Si,* it is a good horse, a very good horse, and you have come far."

The Mexican turned his head toward the house and called, "A plate and a cup, *mamacita*." Turning back to Ruble Noon, he said, "Come, señor."

Noon hesitated. "I would bring my rifle, *amigo*. It is agreed?"

"Of course." Then he added, "My son will see to the horse."

They walked to the house together, and Ruble removed his hat as he entered, bowing to the Mexican woman who stood at the stove. "I am too much trouble, señora," he said.

"It is no trouble. Sit down, if you will."

The *frijoles* were hot and filling; he ate two helpings of them, several *tortillas,* and some roast beef.

"You were hungry, señor," the woman said.

He smiled. "To eat a meal you have cooked, señora, is the greatest pleasure. And if I had not been hungry the taste would have made me so."

She beamed at him, and refilled his coffee cup. He sat back in his chair. "Your road is not traveled," he said, "or else the wind has blown away the tracks."

The Mexican shrugged. "The sand and the wind . . . you know how it is."

"The gray horse," Ruble Noon suggested . . . "I will give you a paper . . . a bill of sale. But if anyone should follow me, I do not want the horse seen. Do you understand?"

"There is a pasture among the willows down by the river, señor, not a place to be found. I will keep the horse there."

Ruble Noon got to his feet, reluctant to leave the friendliness of these simple people. He stood for a moment, and glanced around. "You are fortunate," he said. "You have much here."

"We are poor people, señor."

"Poor? I would say you are richer than you know. You have a house, some cattle, you have food, and you have each other. It is a great deal more than I will have out there." He indicated the night outside. Then he went out, moving at once to the side of the door.

The younger Mexican spoke. "I have saddled a horse. He is a good one and will go far."

"*Gracias, amigo.*"

The others came outside. He had been there only a short time, but there was something between them now. They stood there together. "*Vaya con dios*," the señora said, and he lifted a hand to them and rode away into the night.

Yet now he was uneasy. The warmth of their quiet house remained with him, but slowly a feeling crept over him that he was followed. There was something, someone out there in the night.

He had known so little of life—a few days only, days of doubt, apprehension, worry, and fear . . . and what had there been before? If he was to believe what he had read, there had been a wife, a child, and then their murders. He did not know his age, but he guessed it to be somewhere in the thirties. He had founded his own company, and had been president of it while still in his twenties. And he had been a famous sportsman, a crack shot, . . . a hunter.

Well, he was still a hunter . . . and hunted.

The horse he rode was a line-back dun, tough, quick, and eager for the trail—a horse that liked to travel, that liked the night. He followed the river for a time, and when he climbed up from it he saw the gleam of moonlight on the railroad tracks. There was no sound in the night except that of crickets, but twice, feeling uneasy, he drew up to listen, and once he thought he heard some unidentified sound not very far off.

If he was as dangerous as was implied, they would be wary, and they would try to trap him. If they did not try to kill him now, they must be sure of some better place ahead, some place where a trap would be easier, or where a trap had already been laid.

Did he dare try to escape? Did he dare try to ride out of the basin, turning at right angles to his course and heading for the mountains?

Ahead, he knew, there were villages, and beyond them Socorro. It was a small town but a very old one, a town with many good people and not a few outlaws. The Black Range lay off to his left, Apache-haunted, outlaw-infested, wild and beautiful ... or so he had heard.

Abruptly, he turned away from the river. He walked the dun, with frequent pauses to listen, but working his way through the undergrowth toward higher ground. The mountains were a ragged edge against the sky.

His mind would not leave his predicament, but worried over it as a dog worries a bone. The name Jonas Mandrin had come to him out of some store of memory beyond his conscious awareness. Whatever lay hidden there he did not know, but names and ideas seemed to spring into his mind from that past, where memory lurked.

In such a case, might he not, in time, recover the knowledge of where the Davidge money was hidden?

Or supposing he deliberately prodded that memory by sitting down with paper and pencil and writing a list of all the possible places he could think of where it might be? If he did this, might not the actual hiding place come to mind?

Judge Niland believed that Peg Cullane knew, or thought she knew, where the money was hidden. But why had she not gone after it? Was she afraid of him, or of Ben Janish? Did she hope to have all the money for herself? It took no weighing of motives to realize that whatever happened, Peg Cullane had not planned on sharing anything with anyone.

She was like the famous courtesans of history ... not a passionate woman, but one who succeeded in appearing so; one who, beneath a passionate façade, was cold and calculating. Peg Cullane was hard as nails ... he must never forget that. There was not an ounce of emotion in her, nor any mercy.

By daylight he was among the cedars along the lower slopes of the mountains, following a vague cow trail. He had escaped, or believed he had escaped, whoever might be following him ... yet might not that suspicion be nothing but his own fears?

In a short time he dismounted and stripped the saddle from the dun. He let the horse roll, and then allowed it to crop grass and rest. After he had scanned the country about, he chose a place near the horse and stretched out on the grass, staring up at the sky.

He was a fool to go back. He should find some spring back in the mountains and just settle down. He could stay out of sight until all this was over, and then he could go back east, find a new home there.

Yet even as he told himself these things he knew he would not do them. Fan Davidge needed help, and that was where he was going.

He awoke with a start. The sun was high, but it was not the sun that awakened him, but the dun. The line-back's head was up, ears pricked, and it was blowing gently through its nose.

He rolled over, grabbed his rifle, and was in the brush in a plunging run ... and ran squarely into them. There were three men, but his sudden charge had taken them by surprise as they were getting ready to surprise him.

His shoulder struck the nearest man, sending him careening into the second. Ruble Noon fired his Winchester from his hip, spinning the third man around, and then he was past them and into the rocks that lay beyond.

He hit the ground rolling, panting with shock and fear, and came up with his rifle. A bullet spat fragments of rock into his face, and he fired blindly, then fired again.

There was silence.

The men had disappeared into the brush, and he lay waiting for somebody to move, but nobody did.

Suddenly he heard a laugh, then after minutes had passed, a voice called out, "All right, you can stay there an' rot. We're takin' your horse an' outfit."

He said nothing, knowing they were expecting him to speak; and after a while he peered cautiously from between the rocks. He saw no one ... and the dun was gone. He stayed there quietly. An hour passed ... then another. He judged the time by the shadow of a pine tree on the ground near him.

At last he came out from among the rocks. A quick checking of tracks convinced him. They had pulled out, no doubt believing him wounded, and they had taken his horse, saddle, and food. He had not even a canteen ... nothing.

The nearest town would be on the railroad, perhaps forty miles away, and without doubt they would be right there waiting for him.

This was Apache country, and because of recent trouble most of the prospectors or ranchers had pulled out for Socorro or for some other town. Well, there was no sense in wasting time. If he was to get out alive he would have to start moving. First of all, he must find water, and he must find a horse.

He moved into the trees, found the trace of a game trail, and started along it, carrying his rifle at trail position, but ready to move swiftly into action. He followed the slope for perhaps an hour, pausing from time to time to check the country around him. His examinations were done with extreme caution, checking every possible hiding place. From time to time he changed his route to confuse any would-be ambusher.

Those men might have left merely to draw him out of his cover, or they might believe that he must, sooner or later, come down to try to get food.

The mountainside along which he was traveling was clad in pines, a scattered growth, thickening in places to solid stands. Higher up there were aspens. At first the mountain was a series of long swells, but as he moved on, these became steeper and the slope was broken by a number of deep arroyos. One of these he followed down toward the river for some distance, then worked his way up and out of it by way of a cutback toward the slope again. It meant extra going and a loss of time, but it would make him more difficult to find.

It was very hot, and presently he put a pebble in his mouth to start the saliva flowing, and moved on. He watched for the plants that indicate the presence of water, looked for the occasional rocky hollows where water might lie in a natural tank, even through the months. He found nothing.

He kept on, sometimes running a few steps, sometimes walking a few, and pausing often to check his surroundings. He was making good time, and time was important now.

The sun declined, shadows grew in the canyons, the slopes stood stark and clear in the evening light. He could see for miles over the country below, and far away he heard the whistle of a train, and made out the almost invisible trail of smoke. He felt sure they would be down there waiting. Suddenly a shack loomed before him and he flattened against the ground, almost too late. He saw a Mexican woman, a rider near her, talking. There were a few chickens, and his eyes searched for a dog, wanting to see the inevitable dog before it saw him.

The man's head turned . . . Ruble Noon remembered the face, but from where he did not know. It was a narrow, cruel face with a thin-lipped mouth and a sharp jawline. The gun was tied low. The man turned his horse and rode away and the Mexican woman looked after him, then crossed herself.

Ruble Noon stood up. His muscles ached and his feet were tired. He desperately needed a horse, and he needed a drink.

The Mexican woman was still standing there. Only now she was not looking after the man who had ridden away; she was looking at, of all things, a parrot. It sat on a perch near her, its neck craning. The woman did not turn, but she spoke quietly. "Come, señor. It is safe now."

He walked toward her, poised for trouble, but he believed her. He knew from his lost past that Mexicans befriended those in trouble.

She turned now and looked at him. "Pancho saw you. He saw you when that gringo was here."

She said gringo with a particular inflection, and he grinned. "You could have told him."

"I would tell him nothing! He is no good. I know that one—that was Lynch Manly."

Ruble Noon looked after the gunman. Somehow he knew that if they had gone so far as to import Lynch Manly they were trying hard. He did not remember the details, but Manly was a noted man-hunter and a man-killer who had once been a Royal Northwest Mounted policeman, but he had been fired from the force for an unnecessary killing. Since then he had been a hired gunman for several cattle or mining outfits, and had a reputation as a badman.

Ruble Noon took a drink at the well, then followed the Mexican woman into the house. He washed his hands and face before sitting down at the table. She put food on the table, and poured out coffee. Sunlight fell through the windows, and he could hear the hens clucking in the yard. It was a pleasant, quiet place.

"I envy you," he said.

She glanced at him. "When the Apache comes will you envy me? It is quiet then also—the quiet of death."

"They come this far?"

She shrugged one shoulder. "They can ... they have. Who knows what they will do?" She studied him. "You do not look like one to be so feared."

"Feared?"

"When they send so many after one, he must be someone feared. They search the towns, the ranches, even the huts along the Rio Grande."

"There are many?"

"Twenty . . . or maybe more."

"Yet you help me?"

She smiled. "I like a man who is feared. My husband is such a man."

"He is here?"

"They have him in prison. They will hang him. He is Miguel Lebo." She said it proudly, and with defiance.

"I do not know him, señora," he said, "but if he is your husband I think he is a good man. He wouldn't dare be anything else."

She laughed.

An idea came to him. "You have an old sombrero? And serape?"

"*Si*". She caught on at once. "You wish to use them?"

At his nod she left the room and returned with a battered sombrero, a serape that had seen better days, and some fringed leggings. "Your Spanish is good, señor. Tell them you are from Sonora."

The pinto she brought was gaunt, the saddle was old, but they would suffice. He had trimmed his beard to a mustache and sideburns, and when he left he wore the sombrero pulled low.

He trotted the horse toward the town, following the trail. When he reached there he tied the horse at the hitching rail and went into a Mexican saloon for a beer.

The Mexican who came to the table hit a careless swipe with the bar rag. He was fat, and one eye was covered with a black patch. The only others in the saloon were a peon who slept in a corner, and a man with his head on a table.

He said quietly, "Have you seen the horse I ride, señor?"

"I have seen it."

The voice of the saloonkeeper was low, guarded. "What is it you wish, señor? Only the beer?"

"The beer and a trade. I wish to trade the pinto you

see for two horses—fast horses. I have no friends here,
amigo, and many men search for me, but Señora Lebo
was a friend to me and I would be a friend to her."

"If you mean what I think, you are loco."

"The beer, and two horses . . . pronto."

The saloonkeeper went away and came back with the
beer. Then he left his apron on the bar and walked out.
He was gone for some time.

Ruble Noon finished his beer, and when the saloonkeeper returned he ordered another. Out in front a
Mexican boy was stripping the gear from his pinto and
placing it on a *grulla,* a mouse-colored horse with a
white nose and three white stockings. A saddled horse
stood beside it. There was a rifle in the scabbard and a
gunbelt on the pommel. Behind each saddle was a
blanket roll.

Ruble Noon finished his second beer and went over
to the bar. He placed money on the bar, but the
saloonkeeper waved it away. "Miguel Lebo is my
friend," he said. "But think what you do," he added.

"They hunt me already," Noon replied, "and I think
I can use a good man where I go. Answer me these
questions. How many are now in the office at the jail?
How far away does the nearest officer live? Who would
give the alarm quickest?"

"Only one man is at the jail, and he has nothing
against Miguel. The nearest officer is a deputy marshal
who is four blocks down the street, asleep. As to the
alarm, I think no one will give it but the keeper of the
store over there. He doesn't like Mexicans—only our
business."

"Give him business then. Get five Mexicans to go in
and buy." He placed two twenty-dollar gold pieces on
the bar. "Give them these. Let them buy what they
need, and keep what they buy, only keep him busy."

The saloonkeeper looked at him steadily. "You take
a great risk . . . why?"

"The señora welcomed me, fed me, offered me a horse. She said her husband was a good man, and I do not believe that good men should hang."

"It was a big rancher's jury. Miguel owns a water hole . . . he has owned it for many years. His people came with the first settlers to Socorro."

"He shall go free."

Ruble Noon went to the door and studied the street. It was early evening. Most men were at their suppers, and those who would soon fill the saloons and gambling houses had not yet arrived. A few men were talking, some read their newspapers.

He looked at the horses and saw they were good. He turned. "*Adios, amigo.*"

He walked up the street to the jail, opened the door, and stepped in. There was a roll-top desk in the room, a table, and a chair near the stove. The weather was warm, but the man there sat near it for convenience. He was chewing tobacco, and the open door of the stove was his target.

"Howdy, Mex, what can I do for you?" he said.

"I have heard you are a good man," Ruble Noon answered, "and not unfriendly to your prisoner."

"Fact is Lebo's a good man, but I'm his jailer and there'll be no monkey business."

"Indeed, no," Ruble Noon said, and he produced a gun. "A kindly man I would not wish to shoot."

The jailer looked at the gun, and he looked at the eyes that looked into his. He said, "You're no Mex. Who are you?"

"Ruble Noon," Noon said quietly. "Just tell them it was Ruble Noon who came. And add that Señora Lebo is not to be disturbed . . . nor her water hole. Tell them it was Ruble Noon who said it."

Chapter Twelve

Miguel Lebo squatted on his heels across the fire from Ruble Noon and sipped his coffee. Their camp was in a hollow screened by pines, well up the slope of the mountain, but by taking three steps they were in position to overlook the valley below, now bathed in moonlight.

"I thank you again, *amigo,* but I wonder why you have done this thing."

Noon shrugged. "Impulse, I guess. Your wife is a good woman, and she helped me when I needed help . . . and I do not like your enemies."

"Only that?"

"You needed a chance for life. I needed help."

"Ah?"

"You are a good man with a gun."

"I have had troubles, and men came against me."

"I want you to go to Colorado," Noon said. "There is a ranch where men hide from the law and they will not be surprised if you come."

He explained about the ranch and about Fan Davidge, but he made no reference to the money Davidge was supposed to have hidden. "I need someone there to see she is not harmed, but I must warn you. Ben Janish is there, and Dave Cherry, John Lang, and some others."

"I will do what I must."

"Henneker and Arch Billing will help, but neither is a gunfighter."

He told him, too, about Peg Cullane. He liked the tough, good-humored Mexican. Lebo had come from Sonora and was half Tarahumare, a wary, trail-wise man with no illusions.

Their escape had proved simple. They caught the train from Socorro, and had been dropped at the lonely wayside station where Ruble Noon had first boarded the train on his way south. The same train crew had been with them part of the way, and the long journey gave both Ruble and Lebo a chance to catch up on their sleep.

Ruble Noon checked his Winchester, and his handgun. While Lebo picketed the horses he walked out on the dark slope to listen. No shadows stirred on the mountainside below him, but he waited for some time, checking the night sounds. He loved the stillness, the coolness, the smell of greasewood and cedar.

At daylight Lebo rode away, and then Ruble Noon rode up the trail toward the ranch of the mute. He heard no sound, and there should have been the sound of chickens, some stir of movement, and there was none.

He rode forward slowly, his rifle in his hand, his eyes roving, missing nothing.

The old Mexican lay sprawled on the sand, and he could see that he had been shot at least twice. The horses and cattle were gone. Ruble stepped down and touched the old man's cheek. It was cold.

Inside the cabin everything had been pulled apart in a hasty search ... for what? Had they expected the money to be hidden here?

Was the killing of the old Mexican wanton brutality? Or had they connected the Mexican with him?

He looked around uneasily. He saw nothing suspicious, but he did not like the feeling of the place. Was he watched? Turning slowly, he let his eyes sweep the ridges, without tilting his head back or seeming to be searching. Finally his eyes went to the direction of the shaft that offered access to the cabin above. He could see the cliff, rising sheer.

They had come, killed the old man, stolen the stock, and gone away . . . or had they? Suppose they waited in ambush here as they had at that other ranch? It would be in the pattern.

The moment the thought occurred, he was sure he was right.

But why hadn't they fired? Were they watching to see what he might do? Where he might go? Suppose they knew nothing of the cabin above? Or of the secret elevator in the shaft? They might merely have guessed at a connection with the old man without knowing what it was, and of course the old Mexican could not tell them. In any case, it was a cruel and heartless murder that could serve no purpose.

To observe the ranch with any success, a watcher must be high enough to see the cabin and the corral, which meant the pinnacle opposite, or the ridge to the west.

What worried him was that somebody obviously had learned something about the working methods of Ruble Noon, for they had known of the ranch near El Paso, and they had discovered this place, probably by working out from the lonely station. Or had they a clearly marked map of his hide-outs? Might not any place he chose to go be watched? If they knew more about him than he himself could remember, he might easily walk into a trap.

He found a shovel, and having wrapped the old man in his blankets, he buried him in a shallow grave. As he worked he considered the situation.

He must return to the shaft to get to the cabin on the mountain, and once there he must map his future actions, changing all past patterns, if possible. He must never do what first came to mind, but always something different. He must change his way of dressing, even his walk.

The options his position offered to a rifleman on the ridge of the pinnacle were not many. Perfect fields of fire are rare, for always there are blind spots. East of the cabin, on the way he must go, there were several such blind spots.

His horse had walked off a few steps, and he did not like the idea of going after it. The horse stood in an exposed position, and he had no idea what the orders of the watchers might be . . . if there were watchers. He did not want to take the risk.

As he turned to the house he glanced toward the east. The east end of the house was one of those blind spots. A man could cover it only if he were among the broken slabs at the foot of the cliff, and this was an unlikely spot. The only field of fire it offered was in case a man started toward it, and by daylight there was no escape from the position.

Yet if he was to escape, that was the direction he must take. Turning to call the horse, he caught a glint of sunlight from the pinnacle. . . . A rifle barrel?

He stepped into the adobe and leaned over a sack of carrots beside the door. Earth still clung to them. Evidently this was the last chore the old man had performed before being killed. He took out a carrot and went outside. The horse came toward him, and Ruble Noon backed into the door, catching the bridle.

He was going to release the horse, so he stripped the saddle and bridle to leave the animal free, then he loosely tied the sack of carrots in its place. He hoped it would fool a marksman into believing he was riding low on the horse, trying to escape. At this distance it was possible.

After tying the horse at the door, he went to the east wall with the shovel and the poker from the fireplace. He broke the hard-packed earth of the floor and dug down quickly beneath the rock wall. The stones had been placed without mortar, and one fell from place. It was the work of only a few minutes to remove several more.

After taking a long drink from the water in one of the ollas, he picked up a rifle, untied the horse, and hitting it a resounding slap on the rump, he ducked for the hole at the moment the horse bolted away from the door. He hoped the running horse would focus their attention, and it did.

He heard the slam of a shot, and then another. The horse, unharmed, went racing toward the railroad, dribbling carrots from the bullet-split sack. Ruble Noon lay gasping in the shelter of the rocks.

Down on the flat the horse had slowed to a walk and the sack looked empty. By now the watchers must suspect that they had been tricked, or that he had dropped from the horse somewhere on the flat.

Would they come searching for him? Or would they think he was still inside the adobe?

It took him nearly half an hour of cautious worming through the rocks to reach the shaft. No tracks showed on the trail, and he took time to brush away those he had left. Then he got into the cave, lowered the platform, and pulled himself up. At the top he made the ropes fast, and squatting near the shaft, studied the dust of the cave.

Nothing seemed to have been disturbed, but he was not a trusting man, and he could not be sure. At the door of the closet he listened, but heard nothing on the other side, and opened the door. The closet was empty.

Did anyone know of this place, now that Davidge was dead? He doubted it, but he could not be certain of that.

The cave was lighted only from the opening that looked up toward the sky. He heard no sound but the beating of his own heart and his muted breathing. Beyond the door death might lie in wait ... but when had that not been so?

Whenever a man turned a corner or opened a door he might face death. Now or later, it came to the same thing, but he was not a fatalist. He knew that if he became careless he might die; or if someone came who moved a little quieter, it might be a little swifter, a little surer.

He lifted a hand to open the door when it opened in his face, suddenly and without warning. His gun slid into his hand without conscious thought, and his finger was tightening on the trigger when he caught himself. It was Fan . . . Fan Davidge was here.

She stepped back quickly, and he went out into the cabin, gun in hand. She was alone, or seemed to be, and she was frightened.

"What's happened?" he asked.

"I don't know . . . something. Ben Janish returned last night, angry and swearing. Something had gone wrong and he was furious, so I got up and dressed in the dark."

"Did he come to the house?"

"I don't know. I thought he would, and so did Hen. Hen came and tapped at my window, and told me I had to get away. He had your horse and he told me to let the horse take me, that the horse would go where you had gone."

"What about Arch Billing?"

"I don't know. I did as Hen told me. I was afraid Arch would try to defend me, and they would kill him. There were others there who came back with Janish. I think there were several, and one of them was a girl."

"Peg Cullane?"

"What has she to do with all this? What *is* happening?"

He went to the window and looked toward the trail. She would not have covered her tracks, she could not have, and how long would it take to find them? He went to the shelf and filled his pockets with .44's, then went back to the window and kept his eyes on the trail.

"They are money-hungry," he told Fan, "all of them. Peg Cullane most of all."

"But what is there? Pa left nothing except the ranch."

"There is more, and they know it. Peg Cullane learned—I don't know how—that your pa had some money hidden. Janish knows, too. I don't know if the rest of them do or not."

"What about you?"

"Tom Davidge trusted me. I don't know why."

"And you know where the money is?"

"I've told you. I remember almost nothing, but nobody would believe that I don't remember. I am beginning to remember some things, and maybe I will recall more."

Her eyes searched his. "I don't care about the money," she said finally, "but I do love the ranch. I want that."

"You'll have it."

"How can you be sure?"

"It is my business, or so I have been told. I shall have to play by instinct, and I hope it works."

Silent then, they watched the trail. There was little they could do. He felt closed in, trapped, and he did not like the feeling. The money might be here, but he did not like waiting inside.

He cared nothing for the money, either. He was a man lost, and he wished to find himself. That he was Jonas Mandrin seemed certain, but who *was* Jonas Mandrin? With his loss of identity he had lost the troubles of that identity, and also the hatred of crime that had led him to kill.

The amnesia might be an attempt of his mind to escape all that, and he saw little reason to go back now and try to recover the past, but he did wish to know *what* he was. What he needed now was a chance to begin again.

As they waited he told her a little of what he had learned about Jonas Mandrin, and how he believed he had become Ruble Noon.

Bitter with anger over the murder of his wife, he had drifted. When attacked he had struck back hard, and when the rancher had recruited him to make war against rustlers he had accepted at once, for they represented the evil that had robbed him of his wife and his happiness.

Suddenly he felt angry with himself. "I am a fool to wait here, to be pinned down," he said. He took a rifle and a shotgun from the rack and loaded them. "You keep these," he told her. "If they start to break in, go through the closet the way I did. They'll find it, but it will take time. Save the shotgun for then."

He pulled off his boots and put on a pair of moccasins from the closet; then, taking his rifle, he turned to go out.

She stopped him. "Jonas—or whatever your name is—be careful."

He put his hand on her arm. "Fan . . . you know about me. Don't have any illusions."

"My father fought rustlers, outlaws, and bad Indians when he came west," she said. "If only the evil men are willing to use force, what will happen to the good men? Some of these bad men understand nothing but violence. It seems to me that there is a time to use a gun, and there is a time to put it down."

"You think I could put the guns away?"

"Why not? You were a newspaperman, then a businessman. You can put down your gun and take up your pen. It is as simple as that."

He went down the trail with the long striding walk of a woodsman, but when he was among the trees he waited and listened. Mountain air is clear, and sound carries. Now he was at the top of a steep bluff up which they must come, but at first he heard nothing.

He could glimpse the ranch, but he saw no movement there, nor were there any horses in the corral. That meant that all of the riders were out.

He moved among the trees, ears tuned for the tiniest sound. He was feeling better now. His headache was gone, his senses were alert. He liked the clear, cold air, and he felt keenly the excitement of the hunt. For he was both the hunter and the hunted.

He skirted a clump of aspen, moved through its outer edge, heard a hoof strike stone, and held himself still. The sound came from somewhere down the mountain.

Near the trail he squatted on his heels and studied the ground over which he must travel, looking to left and right where he might retreat. The rock on the far side of the valley stood up like a great stone loaf, with only one long diagonal crack seaming the surface.

They were coming.

He arose soundlessly and moved ghostlike among the trees, where there were occasional boulders and rock slabs. Close to the trail, he listened for the creak of a saddle, the grunt of a climbing horse, the rattle of gear.

Only the aspen leaves whispered in the wind until . . . something else.

He turned swiftly, drawing as he turned. It was Dave Cherry, and he had come up, Indianlike, through the trees. He was smiling as he aimed his rifle.

The gun bucked in Ruble Noon's fist, and he saw Dave Cherry's face stiffen with shock. Ruble Noon fired again, and saw the gunman's shirt marked where the bullet struck.

Cherry backed up a step and sat down hard, a look of stunned surprise on his face, and then his rifle went off, the bullet digging dirt at his feet.

The echoes richocheted among the rocks, died away, and left only silence.

In the silence Ruble Noon thumbed two cartridges into his gun.

Chapter Thirteen

He waited for a slow count of twenty, listening. Then he moved, swiftly and silently, shifting position along the mountainside, choosing a place of concealment where there seemed to be none.

There was no sound. The sudden burst of gun shots had silenced the forest. Even the aspen leaves seemed to cease their trembling. Sunlight falling through the leaves dappled the earth.

He felt good. He was ready. He could feel it in his muscles and in his even, easy breathing. He liked the feel of the rifle, and he knew he was facing the fight of his life.

How many men were there? Ben Janish, of course, and probably half a dozen others. Dave Cherry had been one of their best, and he was out of it now, but they did not know that yet, though they might guess. He had seen many good fights among top-notch marksmen where nobody scored any hits, for a marksman was often adept at choosing cover, at moving. Even to a skilled rifleman, light, shadow, and movement can be deceptive.

He took his time, waiting, thinking it out. Cherry must have left the trail and come along the mountain on foot to try to outflank him. The others were no doubt still on the trail, and there were not many places they could leave it except on foot.

111

He studied the slope, his eye out for places for cover, with alternates in the event he was fired upon.

Ben Janish was in no hurry. He had heard the shots up on the slope, and he waited a few minutes, standing beside his horse. Then he walked off the trail and squatted on his heels behind a tilted rock slab, close to Kissling. "Dave's bought it," he said. "Ruble Noon's killed him."

Kissling looked up. "What makes you so sure?"

"Dave would have yelled if he could. He'd have called us up there."

"Maybe he's still on the hunt."

"Him? Dave never wasted a shot in his life that I know of. Sure, we all do, soon or late, but Dave ... he's a careful man with a gun. He never shoots unless he's got his man dead to rights. I'm sure he's dead."

John Lang poked at the earth with a stick, offering no comment. Charlie shifted his feet and started to speak, then thought better of it. That there Ruble Noon, he reflected, must be the real old bull of the woods, because killing Dave Cherry was no easy trick.

"We going to set here?" Kissling asked.

"We're goin' to wait," Ben Janish said. "If you want to go up there, you go ahead. I'll put a marker on your grave."

After a long silence, he said, "We're going to let him sweat. If he can wait, so can we."

"What about the judge? What's he hornin' in on this for?" Kissling asked.

Ben Janish glanced at him. "He's all right. It's good to have a judge on our side. We may need him."

Kissling was not satisfied, but he could sense the irritation in Janish and kept his silence. There seemed more to this than he had thought.

Judge Niland had ridden into the ranch shortly after daybreak and had had a long talk with Janish, with nobody else sitting in. After that, he had gone up to the house and was still there, probably talking to Fan Davidge. Kissling had the feeling something was going on that he had no part in, and he didn't like it.

He got to his feet abruptly and moved off among the trees. Somewhere on the slope above them the man known as Ruble Noon waited, holding them all here by the threat of his presence. Kissling looked up through the trees. Noon angered him, and why Ben Janish should decide to wait he could not guess. Was the great Ben Janish afraid. Ruble Noon was only one man. He could not watch everywhere.

"I'm going up," he said suddenly.

"Go ahead." Janish did not even look up.

Kissling hesitated. When he had spoken he had not really expected to go; he had half expected Janish to tell him to shut up and forget it. Now his bluff had been called and he stood there irresolute. He could go back and sit down and nobody would be apt to say anything, but he would know their contempt. On such small things are the lives of men decided.

Angrily, he stepped out and started up the slope. Away from the path the slope was steep and grassy, or sometimes rocky. Much of it was covered by trees where he could move from one to the next, scrambling, holding on with one hand, pulling himself up. When he had gone a little way he stopped and listened, sweat pouring down his face.

What the hell? Now that he was away from them, why go up there at all? This was no fight he wanted. He did not like Ruble Noon, and Noon was a threat to them, but it was a big country and he need never come back this way again.

Even as he thought this he knew he was not going to do it. He found a steep path through the trees and climbed up. Ben Janish wasn't the only man who could use a gun. He would show them a thing or two. He had watched Ben Janish, and he knew that he himself was just as fast. What he was not allowing for was sureness of hand and accuracy in shooting. He knew he could be just as fast in drawing against Janish, but what he did not know, and was never to know, was that had they been in a gun battle Janish would have beaten him fifty times out of fifty.

He knew little about Ruble Noon except that he had heard he was a gunfighter, a killer of men. He thought of him in the same terms as he thought of himself, or Dave Cherry or John Lang. He knew nothing of Ruble Noon's past. He did not know that in another life he had been a hunter, a skilled stalker of wild game, a man as at home in the forest as a leopard, and as deadly.

He moved up the slope now, his eyes searching the trees and brush, but his were eyes trained for open country, for riding after cattle, or for using guns in towns or in ranch yards.

He believed that he was moving silently. He paused from time to time, unaware of the rifle muzzle that tracked him along the slope and up through the trees. He had seen nothing, and believed he was unseen. Suddenly he emerged in a small sun-filled clearing where no shadows fell, and as he stepped out from the trees he reached up to pull his hatbrim down. When he took his hand away, Ruble Noon was standing where a moment before there had been no one, and he was holding a rifle in his hands.

"I don't want to kill you," Ruble Noon said conversationally, almost as though they were sitting over their beers in a saloon. "I wish you would turn around and go back."

"I can't do that," Kissling said, and he was surprised at his own words. "I told them I was coming after you." And then he added, "I made my brags."

"Tell them you couldn't find me. I have nothing against you, Kissling. You moved against me down there, but I did not come looking for you. I don't want you."

An hour before, even a few minutes before, Kissling would have said such conversation was impossible, yet here he was, talking with Ruble Noon without animosity.

"My fight is with Janish," Ruble Noon said. "I want all of you to leave the Rafter D and let Fan Davidge lead her life the way she wants to. Her father paid me to see that you left. I have it to do, Kissling. I took his money."

"Are you going to kill Janish?"

"If I must."

"What about me?"

"Go back down the hill, and just say you couldn't find me. After all, it was I who found you. Or if you want to, go back down to the ranch, get a horse, and ride out of the country."

"They told me you never gave anybody a break."

"Maybe you're an exception." As he spoke he was listening, one part of his attention on those others, on Ben Janish and John Lang. "I don't want to kill you, Kissling, but you can see the odds. You might miss with a six-shooter, even if you got it out ... at forty feet I am not going to miss with this rifle."

Kissling could feel the sweat trickling down between his shoulder blades. He had an out, and he was going to take it. Maybe there was a lot of money here somewhere. Maybe. But a corpse doesn't spend very much, and a corpse isn't welcome in the red-light districts or in the saloons.

"I think I'll walk," Kissling said quietly. "You won't think less of me?"

"If you want to know, I think you've just grown up. A kid would have grabbed for his gun and died."

Kissling turned his back and walked back into the trees. He did not point himself back toward Janish, but started working his way back down the steep slope, using the trees for hand holds. He moved almost as if in a trance, his mind empty, conscious only that he was pulling out, he was going to live.

Ruble Noon watched him go with relief. Kissling had been a borderline case ... there was a chance for him, bull-headed as he seemed to be. There would be no such chance for Ben Janish or Lang. They were hardened, and steeped in evil.

Ghostlike, he eased back into the shelter of the trees. From where he now waited he had a diagonal view of the trail, and he would be able to see the men as they came into view. He could get at least one of them before they could drop from sight, and the man he had been would have done just that.

Farther down the slope Ben Janish swore. He had heard no gunshot. "He's missed him! That calf-eyed Kissling couldn't find a saddle in a lighted barn."

"Give him time," Lang said dryly. "That ain't no pilgrim he's huntin'."

But no sound came down the sunlit hill, no movement disturbed the leaf shadows. "All right," Janish said finally, "we're movin' up. Walk easy, an' be ready to shoot. We ain't likely to get too many chances."

Janish moved ahead, and started working his way up the trail. Better than the others, he knew what a woodsman Ruble Noon probably was. A cautious man, Janish had read whatever items had appeared in the newspapers about gunfighters and gunmen whom he might someday meet, and he had listened to the campfire and barroom stories of gun battles. He had heard a great deal about Ruble Noon, and the one factor that stood out was that he was a man to be feared.

The failure to hear anything from Kissling worried him. What could have happened? Kissling had wanted to shoot. He was a trigger-happy kid ... well, not so much a kid as a young man who acted like one more often than not. Kissling would shoot if he glimpsed a target, but he would surely shoot too quick, and probably die because of it.

He knew why Kissling had gone up the mountain, for he knew from experience that it was easier to go than to wait.

They moved along, wary of every shadow, but seeing nothing at all.

"How do we know that he's been up there?" Charlie asked suddenly. "We ain't seen nothin'."

"She went this way and we've got to get her back. Suppose she gets off scot-free and goes to the law?" Lang suggested. And then he added, "You can bet she knew where he went. You recall he disappeared clean off the map when he went thisaway."

Ruble Noon heard them coming and moved deeper into the trees. He was at home here in the woods, as at home as any creatures of the wilderness. He liked the stillness, with only the far-off faint murmur of voices, the sound of wind in the trees; yet now that he was faced with what must be done, he hesitated.

He had been a hunter of big game, a famous marksman, president and owner of an arms company, and a newspaperman, a writer of sorts. And then he had become a hunter of men. After that had come the blow on the head, and the amnesia. He seemed to have lost none of his skill because of it, but he had lost, or seemed to have lost, the concentrated intent, the purpose.

These men who were hunting him were outlaws, they were killers, and if they found him they would kill him, and they might kill Fan as well. Certainly they would terrorize her, bully her, keep her a prisoner. They were his enemies, enemies of society, beasts of prey. And yet he did not want to kill them.

Now his very lack of intent was a danger. In the situation he faced there could be no time for hesitation, no time for philosophical considerations. He must kill or be killed . . . and he did not want to die.

He waited, crouching low, hearing their movements. Twice he caught glimpses of them through the leaves,

and at least once he had Charlie dead in his sights, but
he did not fire. But every step brought them nearer to
Fan, nearer to a moment when he would no longer
have a choice.

How many were there down there? At least six, he
thought. He had not seen all the outlaws at the Rafter
D, and there might even be more, but six he had
detected.

He tried to think of some way he might stop them
without actually firing on them. They probably would
not hesitate to kill or capture him if given the opportu-
nity.

He lifted his rifle, eased the pressure on the trigger
just a little, and took a breath. He let it out easily,
and—

He heard the step behind him even as his finger was
tightening to fire. He threw himself backward quickly,
and took a wicked blow on the shoulder as he fell.

Rolling over, he came up with the rifle and fired . . .
too quickly. He missed, scrambled back into the brush,
and heard a yell from the trail. Then came a crashing
of brush, and above him to the right he heard a voice.

It was a cold, contemptuous voice, and it was the
voice of Judge Niland. "I grew up in the woods, Ruble
Noon. I wasn't worried about you, because I knew I
could kill you myself."

Coldness came over him. He was hit, he knew that,
but he hoped not badly. It was the fact that it was
Judge Niland that was such a shock.

He had been watching the group on the trail, and
had allowed his attention to lapse elsewhere. He was a
fool.

He eased back among the trees. He would need now
every bit of woods skill he had ever possessed. He dared
not shoot at Niland, for if he did half a dozen rifles
would on the instant pour fire at the spot where he was.
And Niland knew this.

Ruble Noon heard his voice speaking confidently.

"Move in slowly, Ben. We've got him. He hasn't got a chance."

His left arm felt numb and he lifted a hand to his shoulder—it came away wet. Wiping it on his pants leg so the blood would not drop on the ground, he eased back a little more.

The steep mountainside was covered with pines or clumps of aspen. Niland was somewhat above and behind him, the others were coming from the trail, so he backed away, working his way down and across the face of the mountain.

Taking his rifle in his left hand, he used his other hand in slithering back among the trees. On the pines needles he made almost no sound as he moved in a crouch.

Something rustled in the direction of the trail, but nothing sounded from above, where Niland was. The Judge was good—he had not lost his touch.

He knew they might be close upon him, but he dared not lift his head to look. He went into the aspens almost crawling, squirmed downhill a bit more, then got up and scuttled several yards before dropping again.

Somebody shouted: "There! I saw him!" It was Charlie's voice.

The brush crashed lower down, and in front of him, and suddenly Lang broke through not forty yards away. They saw each other at the same instant, and Charlie's rifle came up. His eyes were bright with triumph as he tightened his finger on the trigger.

He was looking along the barrel at Noon, saw him there, dark against the green of the aspens and the white of their trunks. Noon was holding his rifle in his left hand, and Charlie took time to shout, "Come on! I got him!"

Even as he fired, he saw a stab of flame from Ruble Noon's rifle. The butt was under Noon's left arm, the rifle pointed with his left hand.

He'll never hit anything that way, Charlie told himself as he fired.

Something seemed to turn under his heel, and his rifle went off into the ground. He stared ... puzzled, wondering why he had dropped the muzzle. He started to lift it again, but he was overcome by a sudden weakness. The earth slid from under his feet and he lay face down on the pine needles. He got his hands under him and started to push up, and was startled to see the ground where he had fallen was red with blood.

He got to his knees and suddenly began to cough. It was a racking cough that hurt terribly. He put his hand up to wipe away the wetness around his mouth, and stared stupidly at the hand. The wetness was blood, a kind of frothy blood. He blinked, and was suddenly afraid.

He knew he had been hit in the lungs. He dropped his rifle and ripped open his shirt. He could see the hole in his chest ... small, and not very important-looking—only a trickle of blood came from it.

He wanted to yell for help, but at first no voice came, and when he called a stab of pain went through him.

"Ben! Help me! For God's sake—"

Nobody answered, but he could hear them moving along the slope, searching for Ruble Noon.

He took up his rifle and started along the slope. He was no longer eager to find Ruble Noon. He no longer wanted to find anyone. He wanted to get to his horse, to ride to the ranch. If he could get there that girl ... Fan Davidge ... she would take care of him.

He made it to the trail, and started downhill toward the horses. He stumbled and fell, and lay on the leaves in a patch of golden sunshine. It reminded him of the spring where they used to go for water back on the claim in Arkansas. He used to lie in the sun like this, smelling the grass, listening to the water.

He could do with a drink, but he no longer wanted

to get up ... or hadn't the strength. They'd be along soon, and they'd find him ... ma would find him. She always had. She'd know what to do. ...

Ruble Noon was in the aspens. The slim trunks of the trees stood so close together and there were so many of them that there was not one chance in a hundred of a bullet hitting him even if they saw him. There was no clear line of fire from any direction.

He got to his feet and ran, ducking and dodging, worming his way through the trees, intent only on getting away. Behind him somebody fired, and he heard the smack as a bullet hit a tree.

He got through the trees, saw a narrow game trail, and hit it running. He was bleeding, and he had no idea how far he could go. But if he stopped only death awaited him.

He ran down the trail, ducked through another patch of aspen, and suddenly saw a steep, rocky cleft leading up toward the crest of the ridge.

Could he make it? Could he make it in time, before they reached him?

He went into the cleft and began scrambling up. The movement hurt like the very devil, and the top of the cleft was still about forty feet up. He climbed on up, and the rocks rolled back under his feet.

From below him there came a shout, then a shot. Rock fragments stung his cheek. He reached the top, rolled safely over the edge, and saw a boulder poised on the brink. Lying on his back, he put the soles of his moccasins against the boulder and shoved hard. The rock moved, teetered, and then went crashing down.

A yell of alarm sounded from below, then a scream. Other rocks cascaded after the first one. He pushed himself to his feet.

He was in a high valley, not unlike the neighboring valley in which the cabin stood. The valley floor was covered with grass, with a little snow along the sides in areas sheltered from the sun, and some snow lay

beneath the trees. The cabin valley was over the low
ridge to the north.

He started to run, wanting to get among the trees
before his pursuers came into this valley. He was bleeding from the shoulder wound, and after a few running
steps he slowed down and began to walk. Crossing the
meadow on a diagonal line, he entered the trees at a
spot where there was no snow.

Glancing back, he could see no trail behind him,
but he knew he must have left one. He worked his way
up toward the crest of the ridge, which was several
hundred feet higher than the meadow.

When he had climbed almost halfway he stopped to
get his breath. He was high up, and the altitude as well
as his wound was getting him. Crouching close to a
deadfall where he could watch the way he had climbed,
he got out his handkerchief and plugged the wound as
best he could. It was not serious in itself, but the loss of
blood frightened him.

As he waited he saw the first man appear ... with
great caution. Laying his rifle down, he hitched himself
into a sitting position, then lifted the rifle again and,
bracing his elbow, took careful aim. He took a deep
breath, let a little of it go, and eased back on the
trigger. The man below had climbed a little higher for a
better view. Catching him in the V of his sight, Ruble
Noon tightened ever so gently on the trigger. The rifle
leaped in ihs hands and the man spun around and
dropped, scrambled up, and fell again.

Using the rifle to help himself up, Ruble Noon got
to his feet and, without even looking back, continued
on. He must be at an altitude of at least eleven thousand feet now, and he had taken only a few steps when
he had to pause again to get his wind. He looked back,
but saw nothing.

He went on, and was nearly at the top of the ridge
before he looked back. He could see a number of
figures moving over the meadow toward him.

Again he sat down, steadying the rifle and wishing for a sling to hold it still. He took aim at one of the figures. They were now six or seven hundred yards behind him; and at such a range, even with perfect conditions, he might be several inches off in his shots, enough to make every one a miss, and the men below were fairly close together—he could put every one of his shots into a twenty-foot square. Seated and well braced, he squeezed off five quick shots. The men in the meadow scattered like quail. One of them stumbled and fell, then stood up again.

Ruble Noon got up slowly, reloading his rifle as he did so. He had done better shooting, and he thought of Billy Dixon at Adobe Walls, who had knocked an Indian from his horse at just under a mile ... but that was with a Sharps buffalo gun, a big .50.

He climbed on to the crest of the ridge, which was half bare at this point. Looking across the cabin valley, he could see the location of the cabin, but could not actually see the cabin itself, which was hidden in the shoulder of the rock.

He was very tired from the climb and the altitude. He sat down, breathing deeply of the cold, clear air. They would come after him, he knew, but they would come cautiously, not knowing when he might shoot again.

The best thing for him now would be to get to the cabin, get Fan, and with her work their way to the ranch. Miguel should be there now, and with Arch and Hen to help, they should be able to handle whatever came ... if they could get back.

In spite of his tiredness, he had to go down the ridge and across that other meadow. Would there be somebody watching the ranch house? Or had they already captured the place? Did they already have Fan?

He started to rise, but his knees gave way and he sat down abruptly. For a moment he waited there, feeling fear within him.

This was too open a spot. There was no place here in which to fight. He did not try to get up again, but instead he lay down and rolled over three times to get off the ridge. Then he caught hold of an outcrop and pulled himself up. He would make it—he had to make it.

Chapter Fourteen

The ridge, the divide between two hanging valleys, had been scoured by glacial action. The trees along its steep flanks were Engelmann spruce, with a scattering of gnarled and ancient bristle-cone pine.

Ruble Noon worked his way carefully along the slope, knowing that a fall might finish him. His wound had stopped bleeding, but it was still a reason for caution, for though no more than a flesh wound, it had weakened him by loss of blood.

He paused by an old spruce to catch his breath again, and a camp-robber jay, drawn by his presence, hopped from limb to limb.

The ground here was mostly covered by broken rock littered with the bare bones of fallen trees, or by rocks half covered with lichen. He found a narrow, steep slide of gray rock and worked his way down, ending up in a thick patch of bracken and lady fern, mixed with scattered clumps of columbine.

He pushed himself up with his rifle and continued on down through a stand of spruce, until he halted on the edge of the grassy floor of the valley, thick with patches of low-growing flowers. He hesitated there, his eyes searching the prospect before him.

The cabin, still hidden among the rocks across the narrow valley, was scarcely two hundred yards away, but the distance seemed very great when he considered that there was no cover, and he would be a perfect target in that space. But here was no other way.

He did not know what he would find when he got there. Fan Davidge must be his first consideration. After all, she was his reason for being here at all. She might be a prisoner, or she might be dead, and he might walk into a trap; but it was a risk he could not avoid. For better or worse, he must cross that open valley and get to the cabin.

His rifle ready in his hand, he took a long breath and stepped out from the spruce trees and started to walk. He took long, easy strides on the soft grass, and aimed toward a point of rock on the far side of the valley.

At twenty steps he permitted himself a glance around . . . nothing was in sight. At twice that distance he was still alone, still moving forward.

He looked at the pinnacle, about a hundred and fifty yards off. He had been a good distance runner once, but never a good dash man. However, he had never had anyone with a rifle behind him when he tried dashes . . . and that could make a difference.

He held to his pace. Ahead and a little to the left he saw the scattered small rocks of a moraine—nothing very imposing, but a chance of some slight cover.

He went on. . . .

A branch cracked in the stillness. He glanced over his shoulder—a man was there, lifting a rifle to his shoulder.

Ruble Noon took off like a startled deer. Gunfire was sure to attract others, and he wanted to be able to shoot from shelter. Whatever running he was going to do had better be done now.

On the fourth stride he side-stepped nimbly and took off at a tangent. He heard the sharp bark of the rifle, and saw the bullet kick up dust ahead. He took another step, then turned to the right, glimpsed a shallow place in the valley floor, and hit the ground sliding, then rolled into the hollow.

There was scarcely room for his body, but he knew how little it took to offer concealment. His rifle across his forearms, he crawled forward on his elbows. He could feel the dampness under his shirt, which meant that his wound had started bleeding again, and he knew he had not much time to get into better shelter.

The shallow place into which he had dropped was only inches deep, but it ran along in the direction he was going. It deepened slightly, and he wormed along until he was within a few yards of the rocks along the far end. He came up with a lunge, and had made three long strides before they saw him.

He heard the sound of a shot, but the bullet must have struck far behind him. The next shot was high, and then he was into the rocks.

He lay down, gasping for breath, but quickly he worked himself up into a position to scan the open valley. It lay empty before him. Apparently they were no more anxious to attempt crossing that open grass than he had been . . . and he had been lucky.

There was no time to do anything about his arm. He now had the desperate task of making his way through the rocks toward the cabin, and the approach was completely exposed. If anyone other than Fan awaited him there, he was a dead man.

Slowly, painfully, sparing his wounded shoulder as much as he could, he worked his way among the rocks. Occasionally he was exposed, but there were no more shots. Either he was unseen, and they were deliberately allowing him to get to the cabin, or they had moved out to try to cross farther up, away from his line of fire, and so come down behind him.

The sun was very hot. His throat was parched, and somehow he had hit his leg rather badly in falling among the rocks. Almost unnoticed at first, it was now giving him pain.

He crawled on, fighting exhaustion and longing for a cool drink to ease his thirst. It seemed as if he had been

running forever; he wanted only to get away, to find
some cool, quiet place where he could fall asleep on the
grass, but it was too late for that now. He had to fight,
or die. But first he must do what had to be done.

Between two fragments of rock, he scanned the valley again for a moment. Heat waves shimmered before
his eyes. He blinked, and saw that they were still out
there . . . four men, scattered out in a long skirmish
line, but coming on.

He might kill one of them, even two, but they would
pin him down then, and kill him in their own time.
None of the men out there seemed to be Judge Niland.
Nor did he see Ben Janish.

As he moved ahead he suddenly ran out from cover,
but he did not hesitate. They would see him, but they
must stop, throw up their rifles, and fire, and in that
little time he could, with luck, cross the open space.
Once into the brush and rocks, he could reach the
cabin.

He took off in a charging run. He had taken three
long strides before the first bullet struck somewhere
behind him. Another struck the rock just ahead of his
feet with an angry *splat;* then a pebble rolled under the
sole of his boot and he fell heavily, losing his hold on
his rifle, which clattered away among the rocks.

Another bullet sounded, and rock fragments stung
his face. He scrambled up, lost his footing for a moment, then half stumbled into the brush and fell down,
his breath tearing at his lungs, but there was no time to
waste. He had no rifle now, and they would be closing
in fast. He got to his feet and went on in a stumbling
run.

When he reached the shelf where the cabin stood he
could hear them coming. He hit the shelf running, but
slowed to a halt. He put his hand across his face, felt
pain, and glanced down at the hand. It was badly
lacerated from a fall on the rocks. He opened and
closed it—the fingers were all right.

Suddenly the door of the cabin came open and he heard Fan scream. *"No! No!"*

A man with a broad, tough face and straight black brows stood before him. "Noon! I'm Mitt Ford! You killed—"

Ruble Noon went for his gun. There was no moment to think, and his hand swept down and came up, and the heavy gun bucked with the roar of his first shot. He saw Mitt Ford back up a step, and then come on; his gun blazing. He was fanning his gun, and Ruble Noon thought, *He's a damned fool,* even as he was shooting.

Bullets sprayed around Noon, but he took the moment given him and put three bullets into the area around Mitt Ford's navel.

The gun spilled from Ford's hand. He grabbed for it and fell, tried to rise, and fell again. There was a widening circle of blood on the back of Ford's shirt.

Ruble Noon moved swiftly to the door. Fan Davidge caught him and pulled him inside. Even as the door slammed, a bullet thudded against the wood.

"Are you all right?" he asked quickly.

"Yes, I'm all right. He . . . he just got here. He told me he was going to kill you."

Ruble Noon crossed over to the rifle rack and took down a Winchester. It was fully loaded. He reloaded his six-shooter, took up another gunbelt, and strapped it on.

After the sudden glare of the sun outside, the shadowed interior of the cabin had left Fan half-blind. Suddenly she saw the darkening stain around his shoulder.

"You're hurt!" she exclaimed.

Driven to desperation by the loss of his rifle and the closeness of those behind him, he had forgotten about everything except getting a rifle in his hands once more. Now, seeing Fan again, he knew how much he wanted to live.

"I'd better do something about it," he said. He dropped into a chair from which he could look out. "I want a drink, too," he added.

"There's coffee," she said.

"Water first."

Just sitting down, just resting there, relaxing for a minute, felt good. What he wanted most was a chance to lean back, to close his eyes. His lids were hot and his eyes were red-rimmed from the glare and from the wind.

"We've got to get out of here," he said. "This is a trap."

"Wait. First I'll see what I can do for your shoulder."

He looked at her. Worried as she was, she moved with no waste motion. She brought hot water and cloths and, stripping off his shirt, she began to bathe the wound. The warm water felt good. She had gentle fingers and she worked very quickly.

His eyes went from her to the window. The open area before them was empty, but he knew the men were out there, scouting around. They had not discovered the place had only one approach. Soon they would know that, and they would begin shooting.

Ruble Noon knew too much of shooting and too much of the actions of bullets to feel confident. In such a place, one did not need to have a target, did not need to see anyone. They had only to shoot inside, through the windows, and let the bullets ricochet.

Many of the bullets would miss, but some would be pretty sure to hit. He had seen the wounds made by ricocheting bullets, bouncing from wall to wall, and cutting like jagged knives. A ricochet could rip a man wide open; any ricochet could make a nasty wound. He had seen it done.

Presently he accepted a cup of coffee. He was well back inside, facing the window, and she was bandaging his wound before they appeared.

It was Judge Niland who called out. "Ruble Noon, you haven't got a chance! Come on out with your hands up, and we'll make a deal!"

He made no reply. Let them do the talking if they liked. He had nothing to talk about.

"We know Fan Davidge is in there, and we know you're wounded. You tell us where it is, and you can have an equal share."

"Equal to what?" he asked.

"Share and share alike," Niland said. His voice sounded nearer. If they tried rushing the place, they'd be fools. He could nail two or three of them before they got to the other wall.

There was silence. Fan had finished bandaging the wound. He was studying the area before him. Everybody was out of sight, but that ricochet business could work two ways. It was mostly open country out there, with some scattered trees and a few boulders. It was only an outside chance that he could score a hit, but he could make them nervous.

"Fan, put some grub together," he said. "There's some gunny sacks around. Get one of them and fill it with canned goods and whatever isn't too heavy. Put in a side of bacon and some coffee."

She did not ask questions, but did what he suggested.

"A canteen," he added, "and some cartridges."

"Now see here, Ruble," came the voice from outside. "We don't want to kill Miss Davidge. You're endangering her."

"You don't want to kill her? You mean you're going to rob her and then let her go, to complain about it? I don't think so, Judge."

He lifted his rifle and fired three quick shots, each one at a boulder or a rock face behind which he believed the men were hidden. He heard the bullets strike, heard their angry whine. Then he got up and put the shutters in place. There were loopholes that he could fire through if they began to advance.

"You've still got a chance to come out," Niland called. "If you don't, we'll burn you out."

Burn them? There was nothing here that would burn, but the wind was toward the front of the house and if they dropped burning material off the edge of the rock above, the smoke would come in through cracks and around the windows. Much of it might be kept out, but not all of it.

He made no reply, but turned toward the closet and pulled open the door. "We'll go this way," he said.

He helped Fan through the openings, and stood for an instant looking around. Would he ever see this place again? He was desperately weary. The loss of blood, the hot sun, and his long struggle to escape had sapped his strength. Without Fan, he would have stayed where he was and tried to fight it out, but smoke was one thing against which they had no defense.

He followed her through the doors, closing them carefully behind him.

Chapter Fifteen

She trusted him.

Ruble Noon squatted by the shaft and considered that. She had placed her faith in him, and he could not fail her.

From out of nowhere he, a lost man, had found this girl, and from the first moment they had been aware of something in each other that was worth protecting. From the first, their troubles had been theirs together. Somehow, even before his injury, he had felt as if he had been retained to free her from the outlaws who had taken over her ranch.

He could have escaped all this, but because of her he had remained, and now both their lives were in jeopardy. He stared down into the shaft. It seemed a simple way of escape . . . but was it so easy?

They knew of the ranch, they had tried to ambush him there. And even if no one waited for him down there, no horses would be available, and it was a long hike to the little station, part of it across open country. They might be able to arrive in time to catch a train; or they might be trapped in the open before they arrived, or while waiting at the station.

By now the others had probably located the shaft. It was not easy to find, nor under ordinary circumstances would they be likely to recognize it for what it was; but these circumstances were far from ordinary. They would have been trying frantically to find his escape route ... and there was a good chance they had done so.

That shaft could be a death trap. They might not have men lying in wait at the bottom of the shaft, concealed in the rocks just outside ... they might not ... but he could not be sure.

It was then that he remembered the dark hole where the ancient steps disappeared.

It was no longer possible to climb up those steps. Rockfalls and erosion had destroyed them, but whoever had laboriously carved those steps in the beginning had not done so just to gratify a whim. Those steps had gone to somewhere, and for some reason.

A secret storage place for grain? It was unlikely. Carrying grain up those small steps in the baskets used by the early people who populated this place would be impossible. However, the place might have been used for certain ceremonies, or as a hiding place in time of danger. Or as an escape route?

He went to the peg driven into the wall where the lanterns were hung and took one down. He shook it—it was half full. Another was nearly empty.

The light was dim here, but near the shaft it was sufficient to see by. He peered into the corner under the lanterns and found what he sought—a can of kerosene, almost full, with a potato stuck over the spout.

He filled both lanterns, then, taking the can and a coil of rope from the wall, he went to the shaft. He handed Fan one of the lanterns. A moment longer he hesitated. He was committing them to a course from which there might be no escape; but without it there would certainly be none.

He motioned to the small platform. "Get on, Fan. It will be crowded, but we can make it."

She peered down. "Won't they be waiting for us?" she asked. "I mean ... suppose they know of this place?"

"We aren't going all the way," he said quietly. "Fan, we're taking a long gamble. If you want to stay and chance it here, I'll stay with you."

"No. I want to be with you . . . wherever you go."

He lowered them down carefully. The platform was so crowded they could hardly move. When they reached the dark opening of the cave, he stopped and tied the rope. After helping Fan to the ledge at the cave entrance, he lifted off the lanterns and the can of kerosene. Then hoisting himself aloft once more, he loaded the sacks of food and the ammunition onto the platform and went back down. By that time even the cave was filling with smoke.

"Will they find us?" Fan asked.

"I doubt it." He looked down the shaft once more. He thought he could see a boot track down there he had not seen before, but in the dimness and at that distance he might be mistaken. He turned toward her. "Do you trust me?"

"Yes," she said quietly.

Drawing his bowie knife, he slashed through the ropes. The platform hit the bottom with a crash, and dust lifted. The free end of the rope rattled through the block and fell to the bottom of the shaft.

Fan gasped, and clutched his arm. Far below, in the light that came into the lower part of the shaft, lay the platform and the rope. They were cut off now, completely isolated.

Two men rushed into the space below, looking quickly around, and then looking up. From where they stood they could see nothing but the darkness and the empty shiv wheel. He could hear their voices, in astonished argument, but could not distinguish any words.

The lanterns had been set well back away from the shaft, and now they recovered them. Fan took both rifles, and he shouldered the sacks of food, and they went deeper into the cave.

Under their feet lay the dust of centuries. The light

of the lanterns threw their grotesque shadows on the walls. The cave was a natural one, but there were no visible signs of habitation.

When they had gone perhaps fifty feet from the shaft they came suddenly into a fairly large room, partially lighted by a crack in the roof high above their heads. Here fires had once been built in a circle of stones.

"A temporary camp," Ruble Noon said. "I don't believe these people lived in caves. There's got to be a way out."

"Why?"

"I've seen villages, probably of these same people, built up on the mesas. I think they liked to live under the open sky. I mean, they built their houses in the open. Back yonder"—he pointed toward the east— "I've seen remains of houses, a double line of rooms, not quite square, often definitely rectangular, and always on mesa tops."

Here it was absolutely still. Fan Davidge looked around the half-lit cave, trying to picture the kind of men they must have been, how they had camped briefly here . . . or perhaps this had been a ceremonial cave, only visited for some special occasion.

Ruble Noon nudged an ancient ear of corn from the dust with his toe, and picked it up. It had been shelled at some far distant time, but the rows from which the kernels had come were still visible. He counted them . . . ten rows.

"Do you think we can find where they lived if we keep on through the cave?"

He shrugged. "There's no village near the cabin, and none down in the canyon, either, although I wouldn't expect it there. These people didn't care for canyons. That came later."

He listened, but there was no sound.

"I've been all over this country, and several times I've found smashed-in skulls in the rows of ancient ruined houses. I think they were attacked and driven out. Over west of here there are some great houses built in hollows under the overhanging cliffs. I think they moved there and built them to defend themselves."

He shouldered the sacks, took up his lantern, and ducked into the tunnel beyond. There was little room to spare, and often the sacks on his shoulder brushed the roof. He counted his steps, and when he reached a hundred, with no widening of the tunnel or change in direction, he paused.

It was hot and close in here. The air was difficult to breathe. He mopped perspiration from his forehead, and started on. The lanterns had grown dimmer ... there was less oxygen.

Another hundred paces, but this time he did not stop. Still another hundred. How far had they come? He had been keeping track, and judged that they must now be about eight or nine hundred yards into the mountain. He was not sure of their direction, but the tunnel seemed to be going east, away from the ranch.

When he had gone another hundred steps he stopped. The lights were very low, and his breath was coming in gasps. Fan's cheeks were streaked with perspiration and dust.

"We've got to keep on," he said. "There's no point in turning back."

He shouldered the sacks again and went on. The tunnel suddenly took a sharp turn and opened out into a large chamber.

"Ruble ... look! The lanterns!" Fan exclaimed.

The flames had flared up, as if the rounding of the corner had brought them into better air. And even as they flared, the flames seemed to bend a little. At the same time he felt a faint, fresher coolness on his cheek.

Hurrying on, they came suddenly to a ledge at the cave mouth. The ledge overhung a valley several hundred feet below, a valley Ruble Noon had never seen before. It was narrow, and the ledge itself was no more than fifteen feet across. The cave mouth was merely a gouge in the side of the cliff.

At the side there was a crack that provided a steep, hair-raising climb to the top of the mesa, more than a hundred feet above. Here on the ledge was a small spring, and they saw that there had been fires here, too. Scattered about were shards of broken pottery, most of them having a red and black design.

He glanced up the steep chimney that led to the top of the mesa. One misstep in the climb might send one crashing down and over the brink into the valley below; and anyone caught midway in the climb by someone approaching from above would be helpless.

"Will they follow us?" Fan asked.

"They've got to be rid of us. We know too much, and Ben Janish knows I've been sent to kill him."

"Could we get out if we went back there?"

"I doubt it. I dropped the rope, and I hope they accept that as an accident and think we're trapped. If they buy that idea they won't follow us. In any case, a man with a rifle could shoot down that long passage and stop them."

"But you're not back there . . . why?"

He shrugged again. "Maybe I just don't want to kill unless I have to . . . maybe I'm hoping there's a way out up there." He indicated the chimney.

It was about four feet wide at the bottom, narrowing to less than three toward the top. Broken rock, all of it loose and jagged, lay along the bottom or along the side along which they must climb. Behind them as they climbed would be the vast gulf of the canyon, its bottom far below.

Obviously the people who had come to this spring, the growers of corn and the makers of the black-on-red pottery, had climbed this chute, but conditions at that long-ago time might have been far different. Much erosion had taken place, and wind and rain, ice and roots had operated here; and once they started to climb, rocks and earth in the chute might suddenly give way and slide right over them, and there would be no escape.

He lay down and took a long drink from the cold water of the spring. When he rose, wiping his mouth with the back of his hand, he looked up at the chute. "Will you try that with me?" he asked.

"Yes," she said.

"Once we start, there will be no turning back. Climbing down would be just as hard as climbing up. We'll have to keep going."

"All right."

Still he hesitated. Perhaps as Ruble Noon, the hunter of outlaws, he had been fearless; but if so he was not fearless now. He knew how uncertain such slides can be; he realized well the danger.

"Isn't it strange?" Fan said. "I know so little about you, but I feel safe with you. I always have."

"I don't know much about myself. I do know that my name was once Jonas Mandrin, that I had been a journalist of sorts, and that later I had an arms company. But that doesn't tell very much."

"May I call you Jonas?"

"If you like." He took up one of the sacks. "We'd better be going now. I have no idea what's waiting up there. They could have found another route to head us off."

"How would they know where we will appear?"

That was true, but he did not underrate Niland, nor Ben Janish either. They were shrewd men, and Niland was playing a dangerous game, risking not only his respectable reputation but his life.

"You'd better go first," he said. "If you slip I might be able to catch you."

He had two sacks, but would leave one behind now. He changed the extra ammunition to the sack he was to carry, and slid a side of bacon in, too. There was food enough for several days if they were careful. The sack would make balance difficult, especially as it could not easily be strapped on.

Suddenly he heard them. The sound was distant, but it was distinct enough. They were coming along the passage!

Abruptly he turned toward the chute. "Let's go," he said.

Fan looked at the chute, and then said, "You go first ... please."

There was no time to argue. He tested a rock with his foot—it seemed solid. He swung his weight to it and began to climb. One step, two ... three.

Using his hands to feel for good grips, he worked his way up the steep incline. Once a stone rolled under him, and he glanced back. Fan was close behind him, and beyond her was the dark depth of the canyon.

He started climbing once more. The top was such a few feet away, but the distance seemed enormous. He felt for another grip, hoisted the sack a bit to let it rest, then went on. The chute was even steeper than it had seemed. Perspiration was streaming down his face, down his ribs underneath his shirt, and his wounded shoulder was stiff. Gasping with effort, he paused again to rest for a moment. Glancing up, he could see the rim, now so close. If Niland and Janish found them now they could be shot like frogs in a tub.

He felt for a foothold, and started to push himself up when the rock gave way suddenly. He felt himself going, and with a wild grab at the wall, caught his fingers over a thin edge of rock and clung tight. Even as he grasped the edge, he felt a hand close on his ankle. Behind them he could hear rocks cascading down plunge into the canyon below.

He tugged himself a little higher. The walls of the chute were closer together here and he got one foot against the rock wall opposite and pushed himself back until his shoulders were against the wall behind him.

Braced there, he drew his other leg up, with Fan clinging to his foot, but helping with her own foot.

He swung the sack over and up, landing it a couple of feet above him on the slide. Fan had her own grip now, and was edging up closer. Using his hands against the rock wall behind him and his feet on the one opposite, he hitched himself higher . . . a foot, two feet.

Bracing himself, he grasped the sack and swung it again, gaining only a few inches. He hitched higher, and heard voices from below. They were wondering how their quarry had disappeared, but it would be only a moment until they were discovered.

He worked himself a little higher, threw the sack and got a good lift, gaining a full yard. He started to turn around, and suddenly heard a yell below. He looked down and saw a man he had never seen before pointing up at him and yelling. "Ben! Ben, we got him!"

"Fan," he said quietly, "crawl right over me. Come on, quick . . . and don't ask questions!"

She scrambled up, and he caught her by the waist. Lying almost flat, his feet braced against the rocks on either side, he literally lifted her over and above him. It was only a few yards to the top now.

"Keep going!" he said sharply. "When you get up there you can cover me with a rifle."

He slipped the thong off his six-gun and, gripping it in one hand, he began to hitch himself up, keeping his eyes on the space below.

Suddenly a head loomed, and instantly he fired. He heard a scream, saw a man clap his hands to his head and fall . . . he fell a long way, his scream trailing out behind him.

A shot hit the rock near Noon, scarring the face of the wall with white slash; then came another . . . a near miss.

He scrambled higher, then deliberately dislodged a heavy rock with one foot and watched it fall. It rolled over and over, fell a few feet, hit a rock, and bounded into space, hit again, and then fell clear.

With bullets smashing the rocks below him, he threw himself at the rim, made it, and rolled over. There he lay still, panting. For a moment he lay sprawled on the coarse grass, his muscles trembling with the release from strain, his mind a vacuum. When he did glance around he saw Fan near him, her face pale.

"Are we all right?" she whispered.

"We'll never be all right," he replied, "until they are dead, or driven away. We are the hunted, and we have gone as far as we can go."

"What will we do?"

"We will fight. We have not hunted trouble, but it takes two sides to make a peace. The hunters like nothing better than to see the hunted come walking to them, unarmed. We have no choice now, Fan, so we will fight . . . fight as they haven't yet seen us fight."

Chapter Sixteen

He shoved back from the rim and got to his feet. They were on top of the mesa in the clear, cool air. A soft wind stirred the air around Fan's cheek. About fifty feet away were the ruins of an ancient village, which had once been two rows of houses, back to back, but was now no more than a few shallow pits and ridges of earth, littered with fragments of the red-on-black pottery.

The wide sky was above them and around them. They stood upon an island where only the clouds were close; nothing moved about them. It was a moment of pristine stillness.

They stood a little apart, merely living the stillness, with no thought of any other time than this. A rattle of rocks drove the stillness away, and brought back with a shock the immediacy of danger.

"I'll stop them, Fan. You look around . . . see what else there is."

He went back to the rim, crawling the last few feet, then toppled a heavy boulder down the chute. There was a cry, a scramble, a rattle of rocks, and the sound of someone swearing.

That would hold them for a little while. No man in his right mind was going to attempt that chute with somebody above him ready to send down rocks.

He got up and walked over to the ruins. Here men

had lived, men in an early state of civilization, men organizing their first attempts at a settled community, men thinking out the rules that would give them freedom, for freedom and civilization can exist only where there are laws and agreement.

The man men called Ruble Noon kicked his toe against a pile of earth. Tom Davidge had accumulated treasure, and men wanted it now who were prepared to obtain it, who were ready to kill his daughter, his friends, anyone. Tom Davidge had excited the greed of men, and here in these western lands men were fighting again the age-old struggle for freedom and for civilization, which is one that always must be fought for. The weak, and those unwilling to make the struggle, soon resign their liberties for the protection of powerful men or paid armies; they begin by being protected, they end by being subjected.

Ruble Noon was sore and he was tired. He wanted no more of running and fighting, but no end was in sight. He looked across the mesa toward Fan, who had walked toward the edge and was looking for a way down. Her skirt blew in the wind, and he watched for a moment as she walked the rim, occasionally pausing to look over. He went back to the chute and trickled a few small rocks over the edge, merely as a warning.

Ruble Noon wondered where, exactly, they were. They had gone into the cave and moved away from the mountain cabin, and they had traveled what seemed to be half a mile or so, and now they had emerged on top of a large mesa. From this vantage point, none of the mountains around looked familiar. Obviously he was seeing them from a different viewpoint and their altered appearance left him unsure.

Already there was darkness in the canyon. When he peered over the edge of the chute, nothing was in sight. He listened, but he heard no voices. No doubt they had decided against attempting the climb for the present, or they decided on another approach. Ben Janish had ridden this country and might know a good deal more about it than Ruble Noon could recall.

For luck, he started a fair-sized rock rolling down the chute. Other rocks slid with it, and for a moment he could hear the rattle and bump as they went down. When the sound died the evening was empty.

He took up his rifle and pack and started after Fan. He plodded along, putting one foot ahead of another with effort. He was dog-tired, his head ached, and he wanted nothing so much as sleep.

As he went across the mesa, he several times saw bits of pottery, usually of the same type as those he had seen at the ruins.

Fan had seen him coming and had paused beside some low brush. "It will be dark soon," she said. "I've seen no path, no animal tracks. Do you suppose that was the only way up, and that they have closed it off?"

He shook his head. "There's got to be a way. I've seen some steep-walled mesas, but never one that couldn't be scaled, either up or down."

Already a star had appeared, for night fell fast in this desert land. The air was chill. He saw a line of trees and started toward it.

Suddenly the mesa broke off sharply in front of them in a V of rock filled with trees and brush, and sloping steeply down. He saw what he wanted, a thick clump of trees surrounded by blowdowns—trees flattened by the wind and long dead, their whitening bones sprawled across the ground.

They crossed over them, walking carefully, and when he was among the trees he cut branches for a bed for Fan on the ground under the pines. Pines meant a good chance that this was a south slope. Most of the trees below them were aspen, a thick stand, almost filling the notch. The place was walled in, secluded.

"We will sleep here," he told Fan. "The bed of dead branches out there will warn us if anyone tries to come close."

From dead branches he built a small fire, and they made coffee in an empty can after they had eaten the beans from it. There was a trickle of water coming down from a crack in the mesa wall above them, and he put out the fire, making sure every ember was dead. Then he placed the can in a fork of a tree. Some other traveler might need it.

He built his own bed well back under the trees. When he went back to speak to Fan, she was already asleep. He covered her with his coat, and returned to his bough bed. Chilly as it was, he was soon asleep.

He awoke suddenly, stiff and cold in the first light. The trees were still dark around him, and Fan was sleeping. He got up, wiped off his rifle and hers, and then went a few feet away from the camp to listen. There was no sound but the distant wind in the trees.

Evidently they had moved well away from the ranch during their escape, and now must be several miles off. Below them, a mile or two away, he could see a meadow where there was what appeared to be a corral . . . he felt that he should know something about that. It was just a thought, the shadow of a memory that lurked at the rim of his consciousness.

He came back and sat down. He cleared the action of his rifle and checked the barrel. It was clear and clean, considering the shooting that had been done. Then he checked his Colt.

Fan sat up. "Have you been waiting for me?" she said. "I'm sorry."

"We'll go down this notch," he said. "There's a corral or something down there."

"What are you going to do?"

"I'm going to fight. They want war, and we can't wish them away, so I'll give them war. I'm tired of running, and now I'm going after them."

"I'm coming along. After all, you're fighting my fight."

He did not protest. She would come anyway, and there was no place to leave her.

They worked their way down the steep slope through the aspens. Ruble Noon felt better, although his shoulder was sore. He moved carefully for fear it might begin bleeding again.

Beyond the aspens there was a growth of scattered pines, and after that the meadow, with grass standing more than two feet high. Beyond it was a corral and a log cabin. No smoke came from the chimney, nor was there any sign of life, so far as they could see.

"I know this place," he said. "I am sure I do."

She looked at him, waiting.

"There's a well there, just the other side of the cabin. And there are horses in the pasture beyond. There'll be a saddle or two in the cabin, and food there, too."

"You have been here before?"

"I am sure of it. Remember, as Ruble Noon I was always hiding out. Nobody ever saw me. That means I must have had several places to hide. Using the same routes all the time would be a dead giveaway, and this may have been one of the places I used. . . ."

He did not remember clearly, and he must think it out. He must try to reconstruct in his mind the plans that would have been used by Ruble Noon, and drawing on the same memory source, he might come up with the right answers.

Apparently his center of activity had been these mountains, and the cabin in the mountains above the Rafter D had been one hide-out, perhaps the principal one. The ranch below where the old Mexican had lived had been merely a place to pick up a horse when needed. This ranch on which he now centered his attention was obviously on the other side of the mountain, with different lines of communication, different sources of supply.

But had this actually been a hide-out for him? Or

was it, too, merely a place to pick up a horse? Or was it a place with which he had no connection?

"All right," he said at last. "We're going down there."

He knew that no place was safe. At any point he might come upon enemies and not know them as such. Even though no smoke was coming from the ranch house, that proved nothing. Keeping to the trees, he began to skirt the meadow, with Fan close behind him.

The log cabin was built in two sections, with a roofed porch joining them, Texas fashion. There were pole corrals and the well he seemed to remember. What he did not remember was the old man sitting on a bench at the door, mending a bridle.

The man glanced up, without surprise. "Howdy," he said. "Been expectin' you. Want I should catch up a horse or two?"

"You've been expecting me?"

"Well, there was a lady here. She was inquirin' for a man of your appearance. A right purty woman she was, too."

Peg Cullane!

"Was she alone?"

The old man chuckled. "Now you know darned well no woman that purty would be ridin' out alone. Not so long as there's an able-bodied man in the country. She had two gents with her. Not that I'd call them gents. If I ever seen a couple ridin' the owl-hoot trail, they was. I'd have knowed those two a mile off, an' they come right up close."

"Did they know you?"

He cackled. "Nobody ever knowed me, no more than you. But those two . . . Finn Cagle an' German Bayles. Two real bad boys. Me, I didn't know from nothin'.

" 'Lady,' I said, 'the other side of the mountain is a world away from here. I never been yonder, never figure to go, an' nobody ever comes over. There's no trail.' I pointed up yonder. 'You figure anybody could cross *that*?' Well, they all taken a look an' shook their heads an' rode off."

"How long ago was this?"

"Two days ago. She described you almighty well, mister. Too durned well."

He was a gnarled and wizened old man with a face that looked old enough to have worn out two bodies. Only the hands looked young as they worked at the lacing of the leather. The fingers were quick, adroit, and did not suffer from rheumatism. He wore no gun in sight, but the bib overalls he wore had a slight bulge at the waist line, and a shotgun stood just inside the door.

"I'll catch up a couple of horses for you." He hesitated a moment, fumbling with his rope. "Now, I ain't one to butt in, mister, but if'n I was you I'd ride almighty careful. I got an idea those folks didn't just ride off. I figure they left somebody behind, somebody with a mighty good rifle."

"Thanks." Ruble Noon looked at the surrounding country thoughtfully. There were dozens of places where an ambush could be waiting.

He watched the old man ride after the horses. Old he might be, but he was far from feeble. His cast with the rope was deft and unerring. He caught up one horse, and then another.

When they had drunk deep from the cool water and had eaten what the old man set out for them, they went out into the air again and Ruble Noon studied the hills, seeking for some gleam of sunlight on a rifle barrel, some indication of an ambush.

"They were most inquirin' about places hereabouts," the old man said. "I told 'em nothin', but the way I figure, there was a point to their askin'. I think that woman knowed what she was lookin' for."

"Yes?"

"They asked most partic'lar about cliff houses an' the like. Now, that was easy. This whole country around was lived in by cliff-dwellin' Injuns. The mesa south of here is split with canyons, and most of 'em has cliff houses. So I told 'em about 'em, and said nothin' at all about the tree house."

The tree house? Ruble Noon felt a little thrill of excitement; something rang a bell in his mind, but he waited. More things were coming back to him, his brain seemed to be clearing of the fog that had settled over it. But the tree house? Where was it? And what about it?

"You've known the tree house for a long time, haven't you?" he said.

The old man shrugged. "I reckon. It was me that found it and showed it to Tom Davidge. We'd been huntin' elk, him an' me; an' old Tom, he put a bullet into one and I went after it, tryin' for another shot. I passed that there tree, noticed somethin' odd about it, an' later I come back for a look-see.

"It was big an' old—a sycamore, an' they ain't too many growin' right around here. Great big limbs all bent and gnarled where they run into the flat face of the cliff. That sycamore was healthy an' strong, but what taken my eye was some sort of polished places on the branches up close to the rock. It looked like somebody had been climbin' . . . so I climbed.

"That was the way I found that cliff house," he went on. "Old? I'd say it was as old as any hereabouts, but this one had been patched up, an' that a mighty long time ago. Up there in that house I found me an old Spanish dagger an' an axe, the kind those Spanish men used who first come into New Mexico. The way I figure it, somebody found this place, maybe somebody who was with Rivera when he come through here 'way back in the 1700's.

"Later, that gent needed a hide-out. Maybe he killed somebody down in the Spanish settlements, maybe he just wanted to git away. Anyway, he fetched up back here, fixed that place up, an' lived there maybe for years. I figure he finally broke a leg, or maybe tangled with a grizzly, or some Utes. A lot of things can happen to a man alone."

"Did Tom Davidge go there often?" Noon asked. Then, seeing the old man glance at Fan, he added, "This is Mr. Davidge's daughter Fan."

"I reckoned it. Fact is, Davidge went there mighty few times until toward the last, when he made a few trips. He liked to set up there, he said."

Ruble Noon walked inside and poured another cup of coffee. It was reasonable to suppose that the tree house would be just the sort of place Tom Davidge might choose in which to hide whatever he had. There were a lot of things about Tom Davidge that might have been explained if one had only known his past. He had the ways and the style of an outlaw, or of a man who expected that someday he would need to make a last-ditch fight. His was obviously a devious mind, but that was not unexpected. Many men had come west to escape the consequences of some lawless act, or to find surroundings in which to begin anew. Whatever he was, after coming to this region Tom Davidge had apparently lived a good life and had built well.

Ruble Noon knew that he and Fan must get to the tree house. There was a good chance it was the place where Tom Davidge had hidden his money, and it was just possible that Peg Cullane was acting upon some clue, or some definite information that she had. On her own, she might locate the tree house and find whatever was there.

"You know," he said, "I think we may be able to end all this. We will go to the tree house."

He did not know where it was, and he said to the old man, "You can come with us. We will all go together."

The old man looked up, smiling slyly. "I cannot go. I think the lady and the man with her will come back, an' if I'm not here they'll search for me. There's no way to figure what they might do then ... or what they might find."

Then he added, "Not even you, Ruble Noon, want to tangle with the likes of German Bayles an' Finn Cagle ... not both of 'em together, you don't."

Chapter Seventeen

Finn Cagle and German Bayles ... he knew of them.
They had been involved in several sheep and cattle
wars, and Bayles had ridden for a time as a shotgun
guard for Wells Fargo. His activities had seesawed back
and forth on both sides of the law. Cagle had always
been on the wrong side, and he had served a term in
Yuma's Territorial Prison. Both men were profession-
als, and they were expensive to hire. And so was Lyman Manly, who had hunted him down on the Rio
Grande.

Had Peg Cullane broken with Ben Janish? Or were
these men her insurance that she would get a square
deal? Or her kind of a deal, whatever it might be?

The thought that had come to him while the old man
was speaking was simple enough. If they could find the
money and get it into a bank in Denver, there would no
longer be any reason for a fight.

Without getting the Davidge money, Peg could not
afford to hire such men, nor would there be any reason
to hire them. Ben Janish might just drift away. If not,
he must be driven out; but the money was the thing.
Get the money safely away from their grasping fingers
and there was no longer a problem.

Denver ... if he and Fan could find the money, they
would have to get to Denver.

But first, the money, and that meant the tree house,

but he did not know where the tree house was. Moreover, he dared not ask directly. The question would
arouse the suspicions of the old man, and might even
create a desire to act on his own . . . or to communicate
with Peg Cullane.

He turned and went back inside and filled his cup
with coffee . . . He carried it out to the porch, and took
his time over it . . . The tree was a sycamore, and it
grew against the face of a cliff. It was very little to start
with, but it was something.

Carefully, he studied the area. There would be a trail
of sorts toward the tree house, but it would not be an
obvious one, for only Tom Davidge had gone there
often. From where Ruble Noon stood he could see no
cliffs, only trees and the mountains beyond.

"I was thinking," he commented, "that Spanish sol-
dier, if that's what he was—the one you figure lived in
the tree house—he must have had some troubling times,
all alone like that, with nobody to help him watch for
Indians. And if they chose to camp nearby he'd never
dare leave the place."

He was fishing for a clue—any clue. But the old man
merely shrugged. "Long as he had enough grub," he
said, "nobody was goin' to get at him."

"I wonder how it was then," Noon said. "Could he
see very far? Were there many trees then?"

The old man grunted. "He couldn't see very far at no
time. Did you ever look at them trees? Some of 'em
must've growed right there for years an' years. Even if
he could've seen past that sycamore, he'd never see
through that curtain of pines. Why, those pines must be
two, three hundred years old!"

"You mentioned that woman who'd been here. Did
she ride toward the tree house? I mean, she might be
there now, waiting for us."

"Not unless she circled around. She went off down
the trail yonder. If she circled, she'd have to come up

the draw an' the lower end of that meadow." He pointed. "An' there ain't much chance of that."

"Well," Ruble Noon said. "we can ride over there without worrying too much. However," he added casually, "we'd like to have the first chance to spot them. Is there any way of getting to the tree house without going the usual way?"

"Might be," the old man said. "I reckon a body could ride down past the barn yonder, then foller around the corral. That would keep him out of sight most of the way. Last few times he was here, Tom Davidge went thataway."

"Thanks. We'll be back, but if anybody should ask, you haven't seen anyone."

They mounted their horses and rode past the barn. "I was fishing," Ruble commented. "I had no idea how to get there."

Beyond the corral they struck a dim trail into the bed of a stream that skirted the base of a cliff. When they had gone something less than a mile the stream curved away from the cliff; but against the cliff there was a wall of pines, and beyond the pines they could see the wide-spreading limbs of a huge old sycamore.

Ruble Noon drew rein and listened. There was no sound except the wind in the trees, a faint rustling from the stream, and somewhere the sound of a walking horse—a horse that walked, then paused, then walked on again.

On their right, under a slight overhang screened by the pines, was a place where horses had been tied, to judge by the droppings and the hoof marks. A pole had been notched into the rock wall to serve as a hitching rail.

Ruble Noon swung down, then moved forward and leaned against a tree, looking toward the direction of the approaching horse.

Fan Davidge got down quickly and moved toward

the sycamore, which offered concealment enough for
two people.

Suddenly the rider came into sight—it was Miguel
Lebo!

Ruble Noon stepped into the open. "Miguel! What's
happened?"

"They are coming, *amigo*. All of them. They rode
out very suddenly this morning after they took much
time to study a *carta* ... a map, you know. I looked at
it after they left, and it was a map of the *rancho* of
Señor Davidge. It showed this place, and I hear one
man say, 'That must be where they go.' And another
say, 'Then it is there.' And then they all go to their
horses to ride.

"Henneker, he knows of this place, and he told me
how to get here fast by the old outlaw trail, and I
came. They are close behind me."

Ruble Noon turned quickly. "Fan ... go into the
tree house and search it. And see if there's a way out.
Lebo, duck into the rocks near the base of the tree. If
worse comes to the worst, we'll make our stand there."

Lebo was wearing two extra cartridge belts, and
Ruble Noon dug into the grub sack for extra cartridges,
refilling his pockets. Then he climbed the tree behind
Fan and passed the grub sack to her.

The gigantic sycamore had crushed itself against the
rock wall, growing into a natural espalier that offered
both a ladder giving access to the ledge, as well as a
screen hiding the ancient cliff house behind it.

Dropping back to the ground, he squatted on his
heels beside Lebo. The Mexican tipped his hat back on
his head and grinned at Noon.

"Have any trouble at the ranch?" Noon asked.

"There was nobody there, at first," Lebo said. "Then
a man came, a big blonde young man. He thought the
señorita was still there. Nobody had told him she was
gone. He rode away then. I think," Lebo added, "he
had run into trouble on the mountain."

"You didn't see Henneker or Billing?"

"Only a Chinese cook who grumbled when he fed me, but who fed me well."

"How did you come to be here?"

"I know of this place," Lebo said. "Once, long ago when I was no more than fourteen years, I come here with my father. He was looking for gold. A long time ago, he said, the Spanish came here for gold, and some had been hidden, but we did not find any. But my father hid in this place"—he gestured toward the tree house— "when the Utes were nearby."

He dropped his *cigarro* into the dirt and rubbed it out with his toe. "Somebody comes," he said.

There were five in the group, and Peg Cullane was one of them. Judge Niland was beside her, and Ben Janish. Lyman Manly was there, and John Lang.

Despite the miles she must have ridden, Peg Cullane looked neat, and as cool as ever. She drew up a short distance away and looked at Ruble Noon, who had gotten to his feet.

"You should have listened when you had the chance," she said. "Now you have no chance."

"That's a matter of opinion," he said coolly.

"There are five of us," she said.

"But only one that's you," he replied calmly, "and that needs only one bullet."

"You'd shoot a woman?"

He smiled. "You've chosen to play games with the boys, and when you do that, you accept the penalties. I see here only four men and one cold, treacherous wench who would betray her best friend for a dollar."

Her anger flared but he ignored her as she started to speak, and he said to the others, "I hope you've considered that. Whatever you might get out of this will be what she wants you to get, and that will be almighty little. Be sure of this: she's already planned to have it all."

As he spoke he was thinking of Cagle and Bayles . . . where were *they*?

Were they even now getting into position somewhere to attack him? Or were they her insurance of keeping the money after she had it? Did Judge Niland know of them? Did Janish?

Another thought came to mind. Who had killed Dean Cullane? Was it Janish? He had believed so, but he was no longer sure. . . . What about Judge Niland? It could be Niland.

Miguel Lebo was out of sight, and it was doubtful if they even knew of his being in this region, for so much had happened so fast.

Ruble Noon did not want a shooting, but if it had to be, he was prepared. He faced them, thinking coolly that he would have to take Janish first, though the others were just as dangerous. Niland, who was good in the woods and good with a rifle, might not be so good with a six-gun. Strangely, it was not Ben Janish who worried him so much as Lang, a cool, quiet man seemingly without nerves.

"Give us the money," Peg Cullane said, "and you can ride out of here."

Ruble Noon laughed. He could sense a change in himself, something brought about by the tension of the moment. He was ready, he was anxious for them to begin. He wanted them to open the ball. He wanted them to make a move.

He took an easy step forward. "Well, boys, this is what you came to town for. This is what you carry your guns for. Somebody draws, somebody dies . . . maybe all of us. Who wants to start the music?"

Lyman Manly edged to one side, easing his horse over, and Ruble Noon laughed at him. "Don't try to get out of it, Manly. I could have had you back on the Rio Grande. I was standing right behind you when you were questioning Señora Lebo. I could have cut you in two, but I didn't think it was worth it."

He wanted to make them uneasy, unsure. He wanted to worry them, to make them shoot too fast, be too ready to turn. . . .

"You boy's haven't kept track of Arch Billing, have you? Or Henneker? That old coot is tougher than the lot of you, did you guess that? He'd take your hair and never give it a thought. . . . Do you think we're alone here? Just you five and me?"

"He's bluffing!" Niland said impatiently. Then he said, "Don't be a fool! You're an intelligent man. You've lost nothing here. You can go back to your own life, pick up where you left off, and nobody be the wiser. All you have to do is tell where the money is."

"You'd take it and run?" Ruble Noon smiled grimly. He was feeling good. He was ready for what was going to happen, and he wanted it to happen. Even as he thought that, he knew it was dangerous thinking. He was an intelligent man and, he hoped, a civilized one.

The trouble was, he was facing a group of people who cared not one whit for the rights of others. They did not want peace, because they could profit by violence; and violence was their way. It was not a matter of what would happen, it was only when.

They would like nothing better than for him to turn to walk away so they could shoot him in the back. But he had been pushed, hunted, driven, and now he would be driven no longer.

Suddenly, in a clear, cool voice, Fan Davidge spoke behind him and from above. She would be on the ledge, aiming through the leaves. They could not even see her.

"Ruble, you don't have to shoot Peg. I'll do it. If she makes a move toward a gun, I'll shoot her right in the face. At this range I can't miss."

He saw Peg's features go taut. He saw her frightened look to left and right. Peg wanted to kill, not to be killed . . . or rather, she wanted the money, and she would not care at all who got killed as long as it was

not herself. Now she was looking straight at the barrel
of a rifle and she could not even see Fan Davidge.

Ruble Noon gave a faint smile at the shock of surprise that went through them all—Fan was here! And
if she was here, who else might be?

"I'll take Manly, *amigo*," Lebo said then. "I want
him first."

Another one! And this a voice they had never heard.
A slight Spanish accent . . . a Spanish word . . . Judge
Niland's eyes were a little wider now.

"There's going to be some empty saddles tonight,"
Ruble Noon said. "Everybody is spoken for but you,
Ben, so that leaves you to me. And I owe you one.
That bullet of yours gave me a few headaches. . . . And
by the way, was it you who murdered Dean Cullane?
Or was it Niland?"

Peg gave a quick, involuntary move to look at Ben
Janish, and the gunman's face went white. "Damn you,
Noon!" he said. "I'm going to—"

"Any time," Noon said calmly. "Just any time."

"*Wait!*" There was sheer panic in Peg Cullane's tone.
She had no doubt that Fan would shoot her, because in
Fan's place she would certainly have shot, and Peg did
not want to die.

"We will ride off," she said. "You win this round.
But don't think this is over."

"Ride," Ruble Noon said. "You can all ride except
Ben Janish."

"All right, Noon," Janish said quietly, "if you want
it that way."

"I do," Noon said.

The others were turning away, slowly so as not to
attract a shot. There were men in the brush and trees,
men in the cliff house, and they had no idea how many.
But however many there were, none but Noon pre-
sented a target for them. They might kill him, but
they would be shot to pieces themselves.

"I'm on the ground, Ben," Noon said quietly. "You

might as well get down. After I kill you, I don't want them saying I took advantage."

Ben Janish stared at him. Then he carefully gathered the reins in his left hand.

He will throw his leg over, hit the ground in a crouch, and shoot under the horse's belly, Ruble Noon told himself.

Janish threw the leg over, dropped to the ground, and Noon's first bullet struck his thigh at the hipbone, and turned Janish halfway around.

The frightened horse leaped away, and Ben Janish swore and swung around to bring his gun to bear.

Ruble Noon faced him, standing wide-legged and ready, and as the gunman came full toward him, his gun swinging across his body to fire, Ruble Noon shot quickly.

One! Two! . . . *Three!*

Ben Janish was on the ground, his gun three inches from his hand, and he was dead.

As the others went across the meadow and into the trees, Lang turned in his saddle and lifted a hand.

And then the meadow was empty, and Miguel Lebo came from behind the tree and lowered his rifle.

"You are quick, *amigo.* Very quick!"

Chapter Eighteen

Ruble Noon turned quickly and walked toward the sycamore. Over his shoulder he said, "Lebo, get the horses, will you? We've got to get out of here."

He climbed up to the tree house. Fan Davidge was standing in the middle of the larger room, hands on her hips, looking around. Her Winchester lay across the table.

"I can't find it. If it is here, I simply can't find it," she said.

But it had to be here, he was sure. He stood there and looked around slowly. Half a million in gold or bills, or in negotiable securities, was quite a packet.

The outer wall of the house against which the tree grew was some thirty feet above the ground. The house was actually a wind-hollowed cave, like many of those in Mesa Verde, and the builders had simply walled up the opening, leaving a space for a small door.

The roof of the cave arched overhead, smooth as if polished by hand, and at his left it sloped down in a pleasant arch, under which was the bed. On his right a trickle of water came out of a crack and ran along the base of the wall for a few feet before falling into a crack in the cave floor.

Besides the bed, there were a table, a couple of chairs made from tree limbs, and a shelf supported by pegs driven into holes in the wall. The floor was solid rock.

The back wall was a man-made partition of stone, with a door at the right. He could see where the older stonework had been repaired and added to by skillful hands.

"What's back there?" he asked, pointing to the door. "Have you looked?"

"You can see for yourself. There's a fireplace, and there's a hole in the roof."

He went back into the smaller cave. Here was a fireplace with a large stack of wood beside it. There were several iron kettles, an axe, some tongs, and a couple of old-fashioned bullet molds, each capable of making a dozen lead balls at a time.

Against the rock wall was an old canvas sack. He opened it and thrust his hand in. Bullets made from the mold were there, of the type used in the old muskets. He had not seen anything of the kind in years. They ran, as he recalled, sixteen to the pound; but the only musket in the cave had rusted from disuse.

He prowled around, glancing up several times at the hole in the roof. On the floor underneath it a couple of notches had been cut, obviously for the legs of a ladder.

He found several more sacks of the bullets. The man who had sought refuge in this cave had prepared himself for a stand if the Utes ever located him. No doubt he had made his own powder, too, and he had probably used a bow and arrow for most of his hunting, saving the lead balls for the Indians.

Where could anyone conceal half a million dollars in such a place? But did he really know it was half a million? Such figures are usually exaggerated . . . buried treasures always grew as the story was repeated. He searched carefully, but he could find nothing.

The partition wall intrigued him . . . it was thicker than need be—measuring at least twenty inches thick.

He scanned it, looking for anything that appeared to be new work. Suddenly he found a place where there was little dust, and no cobwebs such as gather in the interstices between stonelaid walls. He worked a stone loose, and after a few minutes of jiggling it about, he found that it slid easily from its niche.

Behind it was a black metal box. With Fan at his elbow, he drew the box out. It opened easily. Inside were several deeds to lands, mostly in the East, and at the bottom of the box were ten tight rolls—thick rolls—of bills! Greenbacks . . . and they were large bills. Nothing else was in the hole.

"Fan," he said, "there's a good bit of money there. Maybe it's the lot."

"We'd better go," she said. "They will surely be back."

He stuffed the bills and deeds into his pocket, but left the box on the table where anyone could see it.

They went out, pulled the door shut, and slid to the ground. Miguel Lebo was waiting with the horses. "Did you find anything?" he asked.

"Yes . . . though not as much as we expected." He swung into the saddle. "Now, if we had a couple of old muskets I'd say this would be a great place to fight it out. There's enough ammunition up there for an army."

"Ammunition?"

"Ball ammunition . . . for muzzle-loaders."

Lebo looked puzzled. "I don't remember any ammunition. I would have remembered, wouldn't I?"

Ruble Noon swung down quickly and ran for the tree. "Lebo," he said, "get over to the ranch, get a couple of pack horses and get them fast—and pack saddles if you can get them. Don't waste time!"

"What is it?" Fan asked.

"Those musket balls, damn it! They're *gold!*"

He climbed the tree, and inside the tree house he hastily cut into one of the balls with his knife.

Gold, bright and pure!

There were eight sacks, two of them hidden in a recess behind the pile. He lowered them down with a rope.

When Lebo came racing back with the horses and pack saddles they filled them with the balls of gold. Within minutes they were moving.

Lebo pulled up beside Noon. "Where to?"

"Denver. There isn't a bank this side of there where this gold would be safe."

"That's a ride. It must be four hundred miles. Where can we hit the railroad? At Durango?"

Ruble Noon hesitated. "Too close, I think," he said. "How about Alamosa?"

Lebo shrugged. "You call it and I'll play the hand."

Ruble Noon looked back. The trail behind them was empty. They moved off swiftly, Winchesters across their saddlebows.

Peg Cullane was coldly furious. Her lovely features were taut and she rode stiffly in the saddle. Lyman Manly and John Lang rode beside her; neither was talking. Lyman was surly, but Lang was not disturbed— he was a veteran of too many wars. You won and you lost, but if you bucked a stacked deck you were a fool. From the first he had been reluctant, but Peg Cullane had wanted to go in.

There had been too much cover. He still did not know how many had been there; but three to four wasn't enough odds when one of them was Ruble Noon and at least two others were under cover, with rifles.

Four . . . five if Peg Cullane had chosen to shoot, but he had a good hunch she did not intend to. Whether Henneker and Billing had been there he did not know, nor care. The odds were wrong, and the thing to do was ease back and ride out, waiting for another chance when the odds were different; and that chance always came.

Peg Cullane was not used to losing, and she wanted that money. Lang had no doubt that she wanted it all. From the beginning he had felt sure of that. He had been equally sure it wouldn't work out that way. It always turned out to be every man for himself.

It was Judge Niland who broke the silence. "I suggest we stop, make some coffee, and settle down a bit. Then we talk this over and see where we stand."

Peg started to reply, but Lang interrupted in his mild tone. "Seems like a good idea. That was kinda rough there for a minute."

"He killed Ben," Lyman muttered. "He cut him down."

"Well," Lang said philosophically, "Ben shouldn't have missed that first time. He had him dead to rights."

"Ben was too sure of himself," the Judge said quietly. "If he had taken a moment more, none of this would have happened. By this time we would have divided half a million dollars and gone our separate ways."

"So now what?" Lyman Manly wondered aloud.

"We go after them." Peg's tone was crisp. "We go get them. By now they have it, whatever it was, and are on their way."

"I thought you said it was gold?" Lang said.

"Tom Davidge's brother-in-law told me it was bullion, gold bullion. There was some currency, too, I think."

"How come he told you?"

"He hated Tom. He was drinking when he told me about it—facts, figures, places, and dates, and I checked on some of it to be sure the story was true. He got wind of it somehow and came down on me, wanting a share."

"What did you promise him?"

Peg Cullane gave Manly a disgusted glance. "*Him?* I told him I didn't know what he was talking about, and sent him packing."

She dismounted with the others and watched Lyman put a fire together. Standing off at one side gave her a chance to think. For the first time in several weeks she could look at the problem calmly and assay her position.

Since returning from school she had lived in El Paso with a maiden aunt. Their income comfortable, but not large, and the future that lay before her was to her anything but pleasant. She did not like El Paso, and she did not like the West. She wanted to go back east or to Europe, but on their limited finances that was impossible.

Completely selfish, she cared nothing for her aunt, and was impatient of the restrictions put upon her by the small city in which they lived. School in the East had let her see how things might be, and she at once had begun to plan an escape. During her last trip east Davidge's brother-in-law, whom she had met casually through Fan, had given her information that she believed she alone possessed—until she discovered that Judge Niland was also aware of it.

Where there is money there will be hands reaching for it, and the idea that half a million dollars was lying somewhere unknown to anyone galled her. Moreover, Peg felt there was no reason why Fan should ever know about the money. At the same time, it was nearly impossible to search the ranch for hiding places while Ben Janish and his outlaws were there.

The information that came to her, partly from Dean and partly from the Judge, was a shock. A man had been sent to kill several of the outlaws, and he was to deliver the money to Fan. When Ruble Noon arrived in the country, four people there knew about the money: Judge Niland, Dean Cullane, Ben Janish, and herself.

Ben Janish had been told when it became necessary to get him to kill Ruble Noon. The Judge had convinced Janish he must not wait to give Noon a chance in a gun battle, but must kill him at once, before he met Fan Davidge to tell her of the money.

The attempt had failed, and somehow Dean Cullane had been killed during that evening. That left three who had known about the money. Now Ben Janish had been killed by Ruble Noon, which left only two on their side.

She did not look toward the Judge, but she was thinking about him. All her life she had schemed and plotted to get what she wanted, and she had no doubt she would succeed in this, too.

Ruble Noon was her first trouble, but she had little doubt that he would be killed. Finn Cagle and German Bayles, whom she had hired herself, would take care of that. They would also be on hand to handle anyone else who might stand between her and the money.

But now Ruble Noon had killed Janish and had escaped with the money, so undoubtedly Fan now knew of it, too.

"Denver," the Judge suddenly said positively. "He will try to bank the money there. I doubt if he would trust it to any bank between here and there, because he knows we might hold up the bank to get it. He's simply got to go to Denver—and we can't allow him to get there."

"He'll try for the train," Lang said. "He's got a better chance of making it by train."

"And we'll be there first," Niland said. "We'll ride right down the trail to Durango. He will stay off the trail for fear of ambush, and so he will travel slower."

"Where's Durango?" Lyman asked. "I'm new in this country."

"East of here. Animas City was the town, but when the railroad came in they built their own town right at the tracks. That's Durango. It's only been there a few months."

"I gotta friend down the line," Lang offered. "We can ride like hell and swap horses at his place."

Peg Cullane made no comment, but she was doing some thinking of her own. *The fools!* Do they think a man like Ruble Noon will chance appearing on the station platform at Durango? In a town so small that nobody could hide?

Judge Niland brought her a cup of coffee and she thanked him. She brushed a wisp of hair back from her face. "I'm afraid I'm not cut out for this," she said. "I prefer towns and cities."

He smiled. "Why don't you just ride on to Durango with us? It will be all over there, and if there is any more that remains to be done you can just wait there. I will protect your interests."

I'll bet, she thought, but she smiled. "Thank you, Judge. I believe I will do just that."

They finished their coffee, put out the fire, mounted their horses, and started down the trail to Durango.

The man standing in the aspens thirty feet off the trail relaxed the grip on his horse's nostrils and kicked the kinks from his own legs, cramped from being in the same position too long.

J. B. Rimes had come upon them unexpectedly, and although he was friendly with John Lang and was known to Judge Niland, he did not feel it wise to let his presence be known.

They had been absent from the ranch for many hours and knew nothing of the raid that had swept up the last of the outlaws, a few nondescripts who counted for nothing. Arch Billing, Henneker, and a few new hands were now in control, and he himself had been working out the trail of Janish and the others.

He had found the body of Dave Cherry from directions given him by Kissling, before Kissling rode away. That was his first lead.

An hour before, he had heard shots, but by the time he got down the mountain he had found only the body of Ben Janish.

"Two gone," he said aloud.

Rimes had not been living on the ranch for several days, but had taken to the hills to avoid being roped in on the fight against Ruble Noon. He had his own job to do, and it had nothing in common with the work of Ben Janish.

Now he mounted his horse and started east, holding to the path beside the trail. As he rode he was thinking out what he had just overheard.

They were going after Ruble Noon, and they were expecting to head him off at Durango, but Peg Cullane was leaving them, supposedly to go into town and clean up. He had a very good hunch that Peg would be on the train before they were, and that she would be heading east, not for Durango. . . . For Alamosa? La Veta?

He had scouted the country well, and now he struck an old Indian trail that would take him across country toward Ignacio, on the railroad below Durango.

He picked up the first tracks on the slope of Bridge Timber Mountain. Five horses? The tracks were confused, and there might have been one more or one less. After that, he glimpsed tracks occasionally, and near the mouth of Sawmill Canyon he picked them up clearly.

He had guessed right. There were three riders and two pack horses. When they stopped for water and dismounted, he could see the three riders' tracks clearly, and one set was made by a small foot. That would be Fan's. Noon's moccasins he had learned to know, but the third rider was a puzzle—high-heeled boots and large-roweled California-style spurs. Wherever this man squatted he left spur marks in the sand.

J. B. Rimes was satisfied. He was going to overtake them before they reached the railroad.

Chapter Nineteen

Several hours before Rimes found their tracks on Bridge Timber Mountain, they had broken camp there and moved on. In his haste to pursue their trail, Rimes never did locate that camp.

In the last moments of light, Ruble Noon had turned off the trail into the pines, found a small clearing where melting snow offered water, and made a hasty camp. They were about eight thousand feet up, and the air was cold.

Noon's work was swift and practiced. While Lebo put together a small fire, he cut two forked sticks, set them in the ground, and laid a pole across the forks. With other cut branches he built a lean-to against this frame and thatched it with evergreens, starting from the bottom and hooking each branch over a crosspiece as he worked up. It was not long before he had a good shelter from either wind or rain.

"How far is it now to the railroad?" Fan asked.

"Not far now. We'll catch the train at Ignacio."

"You mean the reservation trading post?"

"Nearby. The Denver & Rio Grande stops near there. The way I figure, they'll ride to Durango and look for us there, and they'll lose time. They might take the train, but they'd be afraid if we weren't on it that we might take the next one or some other route. They've got to cover everything."

171

His shoulder was painful. He had treated it as best he could, but it worried him. It needed medical attention, but there was no chance for that this side of Denver, unless there was somebody on the train who could give it.

They went down the mountain early in the morning and reached the Animas River shortly after daybreak. They forded the river where it was stirrup-deep, and a little over an hour later they crossed the Florida near the mouth of Cottonwood Gulch.

The Ute Indian Trail lay across the flat before them, the low wall of the Mesa Mountains to the south. Ruble Noon headed east, holding to a good pace and keeping Piedra Peak ahead of his right shoulder.

"How far?" Fan asked again.

"Ten miles . . . maybe less. With luck, we won't have to wait long."

"I'm frightened. We're so close to the end."

"Forget it—the worry, I mean. We're going to make it."

Lebo spoke. "Dust, back yonder."

"Utes, probably."

"Only one rider," Lebo said, "and coming up fast."

They dipped into a hollow, topped the rise beyond, and looked back. Dust was in the air, but it was far back.

They could see the green line of trees along the Los Pinos River. The railroad was just this side, following the river south.

Ruble Noon drew his Winchester from the scabbard, and looked back again. The rider was gaining on them.

"What is there at the station?" Fan asked.

"Very little. The Ute Agency is just a couple of miles north. I think there's a water tank and a box car for a station."

"I hope there's some shade."

"There is."

She was silent for a while, and then said, "I am sure I have come through here on the train several times, but I remember nothing of it."

"No reason to. It's a forgettable place. The beauty is in the country around."

His mouth was dry and his stomach felt empty. He glanced back toward the strange rider, still too far away to see. Ahead of them he could now make out the outline of the water tank, and of a low building—it was more than a box car. The trees along the river were green. He could use a drink.

He deliberately slowed their pace, not wanting to attract too much attention, and hoping that before they reached the station he could see whoever might be there. There would be a train along soon.

The platform was empty. The small, two-roomed building that was the station was empty also. They rode up, then went past it and pulled up under the rustling green of the cottonwoods. For a moment he sat in his saddle, listening. Then he got down.

"Jonas?"

He turned sharply, surprised at the name. It was Fan who spoke. "I told you I was going to call you that. It *is* your name, isn't it?"

"Yes."

At that moment he knew for sure that it was. For the first time the name felt right to him—not a name he had simply chosen, but one that belonged to him, a name that was his.

"Jonas, isn't there some way we can get away without trouble?"

"That's the plan. If the train arrives before they do, and if they are not on the train, then we can make it. But remember, Fan, they're going to try to get the gold from you."

"Let them have it."

"I can't. Not in good conscience, I can't. I took money from your father to kill four men, but if I can save what is yours without that, then I will have done what it was given me to do.

"And this would not be an end, Fan. You cannot submit to evil without allowing evil to grow. Each time the good are defeated, or each time they yield, they only cause the forces of evil to grow stronger. Greed feeds greed, and crime grows with success. Our giving up what is ours merely to escape trouble would only create greater trouble for someone else.

"If we can get on the train and get away before they come we will have won; but if they arrive with the train or before, we must fight."

He stopped, and she was silent.

The day was hot and still. Over the mountains great black thunderheads loomed up, vast swellings shot through with jagged streaks of lightning. The air was close, unlike mountain air. On the Pacific coast in the old days they would have said it was earthquake weather. He put a hand down and touched the butt of his gun. It felt curiously cool and comforting, and he knew he would need it soon.

He would need it, because there was no yielding to any of them. The weak and the doubtful were dead or gone; Kissling was gone, and others were gone, too. Tough Dave Cherry was gone. And Ben Janish—the top man with a gun, the one most feared—he was gone.

There were enough who remained, but any one of them might die, and that went for him as well. He was good—he knew that deep inside himself. He was resolute, he was fast, he was sure. Above all, at the moment of truth, that moment when it came time to draw and live, or draw and die, he was cool ... or he always had been.

Would he be so now? That was the thing. A man never knew. He had seen strong, dangerous men suddenly lose faith in themselves, either in front of a gun or during a fight, like Billy Brooks against Kirk Jordan in Dodge. Brooks had proved his nerve time and again, and when the Jordan thing was long past he was to prove it again and again—but against Jordan and his big .50 buffalo gun he lost his nerve.

Lebo spoke. "There's a rider comin'," he said. "Down the old Ute Trail."

They could see him. He was coming hard, riding all out ... and in a moment they knew why. The train whistled. It was far up the track, but it was coming.

Ruble Noon touched his tongue to his lips. "Strip the gear off the horses," he said. "They'll go back where they came from."

The Mexican looked at him. "You going out there, *amigo?* Out in the open?"

"Yes."

Lebo's shrug was eloquent.

They could hear the pound of hoofs now, and the train whistled again. Ruble Noon eased his gun in its holster to be sure it was free to move fast.

Thunder rumbled ... the storm was closer now.

They started for the station, leading the two pack horses. Fan walked beside them, still holding her rifle. Little puffs of dust lifted from the road as they crossed it. On the platform their footsteps sounded loud ... a brilliant streak of lightning bulged a cloud with livid flame, and thunder cracked. A few scattered drops fell.

Ruble Noon removed the sacks from the pack saddles and put them down on the platform.

Then suddenly they were there, at the end of the platform, and he had no idea where they had come from.

Lang was there, and Manly, and there was another man—a Mexican, tall and thin, wearing a wide sombrero, twin cartridge belts, and a thin black mustache.

Cristobal!

Ruble Noon's agreement had been for four men and a woman. A woman? He would never have agreed to that.

Suddenly it was crystal-clear in his mind. He had not agreed to kill any of them. He had agreed to free the ranch of outlaws by his own means, and he had been warned to be *careful* of four men and a woman. Careful, and only that. And the woman would be Peg Cullane.

So Tom Davidge had known something about her, too. Now they might never know what it was, but Tom Davidge had known very well who his enemies were, and who they might be.

Cristobal now ... As dangerous a gunman as ever came down the pike. And there he was, with Manly and Lang. ... Was nothing ever going to be easy?

"You can leave it right there, or you can die," Manly said. "You're lucky—you've got a choice."

"The gold's gone," Ruble Noon lied. "All we have here is some lead shot. We got the gold away, and used this to keep you off the regular shipment, which is halfway to Denver by now."

"You can't give us that," Manly said, "so don't try."

Fan Davidge had a piece of the black-painted gold in her pocket and she held it up. "See?"

They did not want to believe it, they could not, but it worried them.

The train whistled again, and the sullen thunder rumbled. Big drops of rain spattered on the platform.

Lebo released the pack horses, and they walked away to join the other horses grazing under the trees.

Ruble Noon knew when a time had come. He could feel it deep within himself, and he took a step to the side so as to pull the shooting away from Fan's position.

"The train's coming," he said quietly, "and when that train comes in, we're loading the sacks on it. Maybe we're lying about what's in them, maybe we're not; but if you want to die to find out, you can have a try ... any time."

"The great Ruble Noon," Cristobal said. His black eyes showed contempt. "I do not believe he is that great. Always he shoots from nowhere . . . can he shoot from somewhere at men with guns?"

The moment was here, and there was no time to waste in talk. When a fight is inevitable, it is foolish to waste time in words.

"Now?" he said gently, and then he drew.

All three of them moved as one man, but Ruble Noon shot at Lang first. Lang, the cool, the quiet, the man who did not talk . . . Lang he wanted out of there, and Lang knew it and was smiling. He saw Lang's gun coming up, rising too high . . . he was being too careful.

The report of his own gun was lost in a crash of thunder. He was moving ahead, a careful step at a time, firing with precision, but with speed.

Lang, then Lang again, then Cristobal. Manly was down, too . . . Lebo must have got him.

From behind him somebody was shooting with a rifle, and that worried him, but he did not turn.

Two for Lang . . . another for Cristobal, and a third one for Lang as the man started to rise, his face and shirt bloody.

Lang was down, though for a moment he was trying to get back up. Cristobal was still up, his fine white teeth flashing in a smile . . . easy, taunting—and dead. He was falling forward, the gun going from his hand.

The rifle behind them thundered again, and then the train came rushing along the track. The shooting was over, and the rain had turned into a downpour.

The bodies lay on the platform like old sacks. Lebo was down, and Ruble Noon was thumbing shells from his gun, and feeding cartridges into it. He had stopped shooting when Lang went down, and he stood there in the rain, watching Lang for signs of life.

People were staring from the train windows. Fan was bending over Miguel Lebo, and beside her was another man with a rifle in his hand. He was pointing with it to a window of the station.

A rifle lay on the platform underneath the window, and hanging over the broken glass was Judge Niland, as dead as a man could be.

The man who was pointing his rifle toward the Judge was J. B. Rimes.

"Mr. Mandrin," he was saying, "I'm a Pinkerton man."

"Not an outlaw at all?" Ruble Noon asked mildly.

"I was ... once. They recruited me to run down some train robbers. We had looked for you until the reward was called off, but I had a guess at who you were when you said your name was Jonas."

The rain continued to fall.

Fan tugged at Noon's sleeve. "Jonas ... the train!"

He picked up a couple of the sacks. Rimes did likewise, and the express messenger took the others.

When they had reached the express car and loaded the gold inside, he looked back at Lebo. The Mexican was on his feet and was coming toward them, limping. His shirt was bloody.

"Is it bad?" Noon asked.

Lebo shook his head. "No ... I think no."

"Get on. You're better off on the train than here. Let's go."

It was a three-car train—just the express car and two coaches. There were four passengers in the first coach— two men together, obviously easterners, and a slender, aristocratic-looking woman accompanied by a squarely built man. The woman wore a gray traveling suit; her hair was gray, her eyes a startling blue.

One of the easterners smiled tolerantly as they entered the coach. "That was quite a performance," he said. "Does the railroad pay you to stage these little shows?"

"I thought it was a bit overdone," the other man commented. "Too much, don't you know?"

Ruble Noon and J. B. Rimes helped Lebo to a seat. All of them were soaking wet.

"Too bad you had to get caught in the rain," the first easterner said. "It kind of broke up the show."

"What do you do for an encore?" the other asked.

Fan was helping Lebo off with his buckskin jacket. His shirt was soaked with blood.

The gray-haired woman got up from her seat and put down the fancy work in which she had been engaged. "Perhaps I can help?" she suggested. "I've had some experience in this line of work."

"Would you, please?" Fan asked. "I . . . I've lived in the East until recently, and I'm afraid I . . ."

"Get me some water, young man," the woman said, turning to Ruble Noon. "There's a pan on the stove at the end of the car. My husband was heating it to shave."

The man riding with her opened his valise. He handed Ruble a towel. "It's the only one I've got. We'll have to share it."

Ruble Noon dried his face and hands, then took off his wet coat. He checked his gun, drying it carefully with his handkerchief.

The two easterners were silent while they looked on unbelievingly. As they watched, the older woman bathed and cleansed the gunshot wound. Lebo had been hit in the side, the bullet ripping the skin along his left ribs and cutting through the muscle. It was a bloody wound, but not a dangerous one.

Lebo looked up at Ruble Noon. "I got Cristobal," he said.

"You knew him?"

"He was my brother-in-law."

"Your brother-in-law!"

Lebo tried to shrug, wincing from the pain. "*Por nada*. . . . He married my sister, and he left her. He was no good. He was a loudmouth. But he could shoot—he always could shoot."

Ruble Noon sat down beside Rimes. The train was rolling south. Soon it would turn east, running along the border briefly. He put his head back against the red plush upholstery and closed his eyes.

There was only the rumbling of the train, the creaking of the car as it rounded a small curve, the occasional sound of the engine's whistle, the pound of its drivers, and the clicking of the wheels crossing the rail-ends. He could hear the quiet talk of Fan and the older woman while they bandaged Lebo's wound.

For the first time in weeks he could relax. Rimes was talking to the older woman's husband, who said he operated a mine near Central City, and had come west to look over some properties.

"... deserved killing," the mining man was saying. "Manly was involved in claim-jumping in Nevada. He always was a troublemaker."

The train slowed, and Ruble Noon opened his eyes. "Are we stopping?"

"La Boca," Rimes said. "Just a station. We take a big bend and go east now."

Noon heard someone drop to the roadbed from the rear car. He listened to the sound of boots along the cinders—more than one person.

Lebo was leaning back, his eyes closed, his face pale. Fan was sitting opposite him. The older woman had gone back to the seat by Rimes and her husband.

There was a faint sound from the front of the car, a sound so faint that Ruble Noon doubted if he had heard it—it sounded rather like the rattle of a brake pin.

Suddenly he heard the sound of the engine moving again, but their car was standing still.

He spun around and hit the aisle running. He reached the end of the car in three long strides, just in time to see the express car and the engine moving away—too far to jump.

He dropped to the roadbed, and the first person he saw was Peg Cullane. She had a rifle in her hands, and she was lifting it to shoot. The second person he saw was Finn Cagle.

The gunman fired, his bullet clanging against the back of the car, within inches of Ruble Noon's head. Noon stepped back for partial protection from the rifle, and then as Peg fired he ran forward three quick, short steps, stopped, and shot from the hip. The bullet spun Cagle around, throwing him off balance. Dropping to one knee, Noon laid the barrel of his gun across his left forearm and shot again, and Cagle backed up and fell.

Two rifle shots spat sand and dirt in front of Noon, and then a shot came from the train.

The engine and express car had stopped. He saw that Finn Cagle was getting up, and shot into him again. Somebody shot from the car behind him, and he saw Peg Cullane drop her rifle.

Ruble Noon ran forward. Suddenly he heard the drivers spin as the power was thrown to the engine and he jumped for the rear of the express car.

He grabbed the door and ripped it open. The express messenger lay sprawled on the floor, his scalp laid open from a blow. The gold was still there in its neat sacks. He ran the length of the car, loading three chambers as he ran, and scrambled up on the tender.

Bayles, the one who ran with Cagle, turned sharply as the coal rattled and threw up his gun for a shot. The engineer lunged into him, and Bayles fell from the train, hitting the edge of the roadbed and rolling over into the grass and pine needles alongside the track.

He sprang to his feet, staggered, and the stagger made Noon miss his first shot. He swung to the ground and they faced each other.

Bayles was badly shaken, and the side of his face was bleeding from hitting the ground, but he still gripped his gun.

"Ruble Noon, is it?" he said. "I've heard of you. Now it's you an' me."

"You can drop it and ride out," Noon said, "and it can end here."

"You joke. You think I will end it so? I am not afraid of you, Ruble Noon. German Bayles has killed his men, too."

"We'd both be better off at some other occupation," Ruble Noon replied calmly. "Enough men have died."

"Sooner or later we all die. I think it is your time now, Ruble Noon. I think tomorrow in the saloons they will be telling how German Bayles killed you ... face to face beside the railroad tracks."

"Cagle's had it," Noon said. "He's dead, or close to it."

"And now—" Bayles's gun was in his hand, and so was Ruble Noon's. Both men fired at the same instant. Noon felt the bullet strike him, felt his leg buckle under him, and he went down.

He was still shooting, but Bayles was walking in, smiling, confident. "Tomorrow in the saloons they will be talking, he said, "talking of how ..." He fired again as he spoke, and Ruble Noon's body jerked with the shock of the bullet. "... of how German Bayles killed Ruble Noon ... the great Ruble Noon." The words came out slowly.

Ruble Noon was down, his brain a dizzy buzzing, his body numb. He tried to rise as German Bayles came toward him, but his leg refused to function.

Bayles was lifting his pistol for a final shot. The sun was hot on his face, a white cloud was drifting behind Bayles's head; Noon could hear the crunch of gravel and the whisper of the coarse weeds as Bayles came on.

He noticed with surprise that there was blood on Bayles's shirt ... he did not remember hitting him ... and the German's face was beginning to streak with blood from a scalp wound. He was coming in close, still smiling. He stopped and spread his legs, seeming to waver just a little.

Ruble Noon saw the dirty blue of Bayles's shirt, saw the gun coming level, and then he fired twice, and heard the gun click on an empty chamber.

He flicked open the loading gate with his thumb, but he was lying on his elbow and he could not bring the other hand into play, so he tried to sit up, and failed. Bayles fell heavily beside him.

Ruble Noon rolled over on the hot gravel, smelling the dusty smell of the weeds, and he worked the ejector rod and thrust out a shell, loading the cartridge in its place.

He spun the cylinder and looked over at Bayles. The German was staring at him, smiling. "Tomorrow in the saloons . . . they will be saying . . ." His voice trailed off, but he still looked at Ruble Noon.

"You are a good man, Ruble Noon," he was saying, ". . . a good man . . . with a gun. . . ."

He was still smiling—and he was dead.

Ruble Noon tried to get up. He heard running feet, and then hands caught him and he felt himself eased back to the ground.

"He's hit hard," someone said, a cool, woman's voice, "I used to help my father—he was an Army surgeon. I think he knew more about bullet wounds than any man alive."

Wind brushed his face. His eyes opened and he looked at a curtain, a white, lacy curtain at a window that looked out on green grass. Everything was peaceful and still.

He lifted his hand to his face. Just then someone came in the door. It was Fan.

"Where are we?" he asked.

"In Alamosa. You've had a hard time of it, Jonas."

"How long have I been here?"

"Two weeks. Mrs. McClain stayed on to help you through the worst of it. She said the doctor was incompetent. She left just last night."

"I'd like to thank her."

"You did, a number of times."

He was silent for a while, and then he said, "Who shot Peg Cullane? You?"

"Rimes. He shot at her gun, and he was not far off. He was using a rifle, you know. She lost two fingers."

"I'm sorry."

"I'm not. She was asking for trouble."

The curtain blew a little in the wind. The air was cool and pleasant. He felt tired, but at the same time he felt good.

"I want to go back," he said.

"Back east?"

"Back to the Rafter D. That's a good outfit—and run the right way . . ."

He closed his eyes, and in his mind he could see the late snow on the ridge near the high cabin, and the way the grass bent before the wind in the meadows back of the ranch house.

"All right," she said.

ABOUT THE AUTHOR

LOUIS L'AMOUR, born Louis Dearborn L'Amour, is of French-Irish descent. Although Mr. L'Amour claims his writing began as a "spur-of-the-moment thing," prompted by friends who relished his verbal tales of the West, he comes by his talent honestly. A frontiersman by heritage (his grandfather was scalped by the Sioux), and a universal man by experience, Louis L'Amour lives the life of his fictional heroes. Since leaving his native Jamestown, North Dakota, at the age of fifteen, he's been a longshoreman, lumberjack, elephant handler, hay shocker, flume builder, fruit picker, and an officer on tank destroyers during World War II. And he's written four hundred short stories and over fifty books (including a volume of poetry).

Mr. L'Amour has lectured widely, traveled the West thoroughly, studied archaeology, compiled biographies of over one thousand Western gunfighters, and read prodigiously (his library holds more than two thousand volumes). And he's watched thirty-one of his westerns as movies. He's circled the world on a freighter, mined in the West, sailed a dhow on the Red Sea, been shipwrecked in the West Indies, stranded in the Mojave Desert. He's won fifty-one of fifty-nine fights as a professional boxer and pinch-hit for Dorothy Kilgallen when she was on vacation from her column. Since 1816, thirty-three members of his family have been writers. And, he says, "I could sit in the middle of Sunset Boulevard and write with my typewriter on my knees; temperamental I am not."

Mr. L'Amour is re-creating an 1865 Western town, christened Shalako, where the borders of Utah, Arizona, New Mexico, and Colorado meet. Historically authentic from whistle to well, it will be a live, operating town, as well as a movie location and tourist attraction.

Mr. L'Amour now lives in Los Angeles with his wife Kathy, who helps with the enormous amount of research he does for his books. Soon, Mr. L'Amour hopes, the children (Beau and Angelique) will be helping too.

BANTAM'S #1
ALL-TIME BESTSELLING AUTHOR
AMERICA'S FAVORITE WESTERN WRITER

☐	12354	BENDIGO SHAFTER	$2.25
☐	13881	THE KEY-LOCK MAN	$1.95
☐	13719	RADIGAN	$1.95
☐	13609	WAR PARTY	$1.95
☐	13882	KIOWA TRAIL	$1.95
☐	13683	THE BURNING HILLS	$1.95
☐	12064	SHALAKO	$1.75
☐	13680	KILRONE	$1.95
☐	13794	THE RIDER OF LOST CREEK	$1.95
☐	13798	CALLAGHEN	$1.95
☐	14114	THE QUICK AND THE DEAD	$1.95
☐	12729	OVER ON THE DRY SIDE	$1.75
☐	13722	DOWN THE LONG HILLS	$1.95
☐	13240	WESTWARD THE TIDE	$1.75
☐	12043	KID RODELO	$1.75
☐	12887	BROKEN GUN	$1.75
☐	13898	WHERE THE LONG GRASS BLOWS	$1.95
☐	12519	HOW THE WEST WAS WON	$1.75

Buy them at your local bookstore or use this
handy coupon for ordering: